I0788418

NEW DAWNING

MARC SAPORITO

DANIEL RUSSOMANO

ACKNOWLEDGEMENTS

Marc Saporito

First off, to my seven Amazing Children, Tara Marie, Dean Anthony, Marc John Jr, Dante Nicholas, Ava Lauren, And Hailey Joy… And Alexa Joy, who is watching us all from heaven!!! Gone but never forgotten! This is why I push so hard with everything I do because you all give me the strength to move through every day whether you know it or not!!! I love you all so much. Never forget that!!!

To my Wife, Allison, through good times and bad times, I always know there is and always will be something special between us, and I do always appreciate everything that you've done for me. Much Love to you Always!!!

My brothers Tony and Paul for Always sticking up for me in my endeavors and for your never-ending support much love to you both always!! And also, I can't forget my brother Tony's wife, my sister-in-law Cecelia for all her constant help during my times of need. Much love, and last but not least, Mr. Daniel Russomano, my CFO and writing counterpart, you always hear me say, I couldn't have done this without you, my brother much Love, my Friend!!! Now's the time to show the world what New Dawning and Its sequel is all about!!!

ACKNOWLEDGEMENTS

Daniel Russomano

To my son Daniel, you are my inspiration; you are and always will be the best thing that ever happened to me. I'm so proud to be your Dad!!

To my Daughter-in-law Lindsay, I love you like you're my own daughter!! Thank you for coming into our lives. You are the best!!!

To my Granddaughter Mila!! You make my world a better place!! You make everyday special!! You are always in my heart!!!

To my Granddaughter Paige!! At the time of writing this novel, I am still waiting for your arrival. I can't wait to see your beautiful smile!!!

To my Granddaughter Alexa Ray!! You left us way too soon, play with the Angels, my beautiful girl!!!

PREFACE

LOVE KNOWS NO BOUNDARIES Especially for twenty-two-year-old Felice Levito, who is being questioned in a Chicago police station about her story and life to a police sergeant and her childhood friend, vigilante gangbanger Tommy Cade. Felice and Tommy's sometimes turbulent relationship began when they were both age six, where the Levitos and Cades lived right next door to each other in a town called Belleville, New Jersey. As children, both were inseparable; Tommy was a very strikingly handsome young boy, sometimes uncontrollable, always getting into trouble in and out of school. Felice, on the other hand, a blonde-haired blue-eyed cutie but a quite shy Tommy's silent partner in crime, always by his side but even at her early age, had a knack of pulling Tommy back so he wouldn't get into any serious trouble sometimes she was successful other times not so much Felice was at that age very mature for her age, and one thing was certain she always had a huge crush on Tommy. Anyway, fights were common in the Cade household. Tommy's adoptive parents, Steve, and Renee Cade, fought about everything, including bills, jealousy, and especially about Tommy. Steve, a truck driver, always resented the fact that Renee adopted Tommy while Steve spent months on the road leaving Renee at home alone and not consulting with him first about it, also dashing his dreams of becoming a pro boxer. And settled for a cross-country truck driver's job to support his family. As a result, Renee resented Steve for taking this job, not wanting to be around much, and not loving her as much as she needed him to. But as time went on and the rare times, they did have time for one another; they had a biological daughter, Nicole, who was the apple of Steve's eye after he grew up a bit and settled down, taking only local truck job runs. But even though Renee stuck it out with Steve, their relationship was never a good one, and Tommy was always the bastard son.

On the other hand, Felice's parents were stable when she was a young girl, instilling moral values in their daughter. Thus, until Felice became a teen here, a lot of cracks in their relationship began to show. Frank, Felice's father, had a huge gambling problem leaving her mother, Sandra, to take care of their family finances and their daughter on her own. Sandra took to drinking and had numerous affairs, leaving a young Felice feeling resentful and confused by both of her parents, forcing her to leave home and take off to Chicago with her friends to search for an Art career.......

This is where Tommy and Felice's story begins and how a small twist of fate brought them together again.

ONE

Felice's side

Chicago present day, A cloudy Saturday afternoon, a police sergeant sits on the edge of his desk awaiting a young woman named Felice Levito to tell her story and get the information he needs about her relationship with Tommy Cade, her friend, turned lover, turned husband, part of a brutal vigilante street gang called the East Street Thunder. Her mother, Sandra, sits by her daughter and tries to console her as best as she can. Her father, Frank, is there also leaning up against the wall growing restless, awaiting what he feels about the interrogation of his daughter to begin. The Police Sergeant begins, "Okay, Felice, I know this is quite hard for you, but just tell your story slowly, and we will get through this, okay?" Felice, teary-eyed, nods her head. "Yes, Tommy and I have been friends since we were kids..." Sandra, rubbing Felice's shoulders, cuts in. "Tommy and his family lived next door to us back in New Jersey." Felice looked away, out the window. "Anyway, we were like brother and sister for a time. Wherever Tommy was, you can rest assured I wasn't too far behind him."

"Remember, Mom?" Felice says with a sad smile on her face. "At that time, you thought I would become a follower, not a leader. You were worried that I didn't have my own identity." Sandra replies, "I remember." Felice continues to stare out the window, going into a flashback of images in her head. "Sure, we fought and all, but we worked it out all the time. I can never forget the day before he moved away. My mom and dad gathered everyone around the neighborhood, including Tommy and his family, and we had a going away party for them. That day was so nice! I remember it like it was yesterday."

Everyone we knew was laughing, crying, and singing, and I remember Tommy grabbing me and pulling me into the house and the basement. Felice cannot hold back her tears anymore and begins to cry. We were both laughing and giggling, and then he kissed me. Then he looked at me and said we would meet again somewhere, some place. Now remember, we were no more than seven or eight at that time, but if you met Tommy, you would believe and trust him. At times he could be very scary but always trustworthy; you could count on him. The Sargent breaks in, "I see. Where did you meet up with Tommy again? Can you tell me more about that?" This bothers Felice a lot, but she nods, "Ok."

At this particular time, I was seeing this guy. His name was Richie. I didn't see it at the time, but he was a total "ass" to me, anyway. We were at some club where all kinds of people were hanging out while the music was blasting. We all had a little too much to drink. I was talking to one of my friends. I turned around, and there went Richie off with somebody else; at this point, I didn't even care that much. I've seen the back of his hand one time too many, anyway. I thought I loved him even after all that! Huh, but that all changed when I ran into Tommy again. Felice goes into her mother's arms, "Oh, Mom, I loved him so much!" Felice takes a short pause for a moment and continues to cry.

There was something going around in the club that two rival street gangs were mixed in. One was named "The Killa Dogs" and the other was "E-6 Thunder" E-6 was the gang Tommy belonged to. Tommy was there all that time, and I didn't even know it. My friends and I weren't that concerned about getting in trouble because my friend Ashlie knew a few guys from E-6, and they assured us if anything went down between the two gangs, they would get us out of there fast! Felice continues to talk as her mind drifts back into the past...

TWO

Felice's side
(Pt. Two)

Felice continues... After the club closed, the party continued at Ashlie's apartment, where I was staying. It's a wonder we didn't get kicked out of there with all the noise and commotion. I haven't seen Richie all night, and I was a bit concerned, not because I was worried about who he was with, but with the gang activity at the club and all. I still didn't want him to get hurt if he shot his mouth off to anybody. I asked Ashlie if she had seen him, and she said, "No." Five minutes later, I turned around and saw him walking out of the bedroom. Richie was drunk as anything with two Tramps on his arm, and he walked past me and said, "Too bad you couldn't join us, Felice; maybe next time?" The three of them laughed, walked right past me, and walked right out the front door. Ashlie turned to me and gave me a hug and said it all was going to be alright. I made up my mind that night that Richie or no one would make a fool of me anymore. "I've had it!"

THREE

Tommy's side

In Ashlie's building, in it is a large stairwell, and sitting there is a young guy. This is Tommy Twenty-Three. A good-looking guy with brown hair, blue eyes, and a medium build. He sits slouched on the steps, looks like he was drinking a bit too much, and mumbles to himself, "What a fuckin" life. There's got to be more!" At this time, another E-6 thunder gang member, "Stats," comes walking out with a bottle of whiskey. He stands in front of Tommy, "What's up, Tommy? How's life treating you?" Tommy looks up and replies, "Hey, Stats, I got to get the hell out of here, bro! Back to roots, ya know?" Tommy pulls the bottle of whiskey out of Stat's hand, "Give me some of this," and then Tommy laughs. He tries to get up off the steps but can't at the moment and then sits back down. Stats then grabs the whiskey bottle back from Tommy, bends down in front of him, and says, "Words inside that there are Killa dogs mixed in there, but they're not flying their colors. If so, there looking to start something tonight." Tommy laughs and replies, "Ha, The Killa pussies, fuck them. I'm more interested in the snatch situation in there!" Stats replies, "Just come in and see what one you want to get it in with!" Stats helps an intoxicated Tommy up the steps.

FOUR

Ashlie's Apartment
(The After Party)

Inside, things are beginning to heat up. The music blares loud enough that some people, at first, are preoccupied to notice that a gang battle is about to ensue; some go off into the bedrooms, others drink, and some dance. Felice and Ashlie are in the kitchen, where Ashlie continues to console Felice about Richie. In the living room, one of the head members of E-6, named "Big Vic," spots a Killa Dog member touching one of Ashlie's friends that doesn't want to be bothered. But as she continues to tell him to leave her alone, he gets very angered and throws her up against the wall, puts his hand up her skirt and rips her panties off, and tries to have sex with her; the young woman screams. Big Vic sees this and runs over to them, and a shouting match begins. The Killa Dog getting in Big Vic's face, "What you gonna do about it, bitch? Mind you own fuckin' business." Big Vic replies, "This is my fuckin' business!" The two shout so loud that it drowns out the music. Some people begin to scatter out the door. At this time, Tommy and Stats walk into the room and immediately go to E-6's side. Both gangs part to their sides and begin to taunt each other.

Big Vic pulls Ashlie's friend away in the back of E-6. She screams as guns are drawn. Tommy now grabs one of the Killa Dogs and begins to beat him severely; the fighting goes on for a while, and gunshots are fired. People who were in the rooms now run out in terror to safety. Felice and Ashlie, who are in the kitchen, use the fire escape to get out, helping others that could not get out through the Living Room; as Ashlie goes out the window, she cries, "My House is trashed, damn it! I hope I know one is dead in there!" Inside, the fight rages until the Landlord rushes upstairs with the police.

Both gangs scatter, pushing and punching their way through the police; once outside, police officers chase and round up as many gang members as possible. Tommy is one of them; two officers grab and throw Tommy to the ground. Tommy shouts to them, "What, are you, a bunch of pussies? Get these motherfucking things off of me!"

FIVE

The Police Department

The room is crowded with E-6 and Killa Dog gangbangers, in cuffs sitting on opposite sides of one another. Police are having a very hard time controlling them all. Also, the other civilians at the after-party, Felice and Ashlie, who were also picked up by the police, sit in the back of the room. Two Police officers now bring a very disorderly Tommy in who shouts at them, "Get your fuckin' hands off me, Five O'! You don't understand! One of those "Punk Asses" was going to molest somebody at the party, and we were going to give the mother fucker a beating he would never forget! Where were you fuckers? Eating donuts?" members of E-6 laugh and call out Tommy's name "TOMMY!!!"

The Police lieutenant is at his desk with a pad and pen, "Okay, Pierce, you can start calling off names now!" The Officer who has Tommy responds, "Lieutenant, I have one more over here!" The lieutenant says, "Put that piece of garbage in the back of the room! A drunken Tommy laughs as the Officer sits him in the back and sits him right next to Felice, but the two don't recognize each other yet. The Police officer calls off names; Felice, who doesn't have a jacket, begins to shiver. She turns to Ashlie. It's really cold in here, isn't it? Tommy turns and looks at Felice. Ashlie nods her head. "Yeah, it is. They won't keep us here that long." Tommy listens to the two girls talk, takes off his jacket, and hands Felice his jacket. He wraps the jacket around her shoulders, "Here, take my jacket!!" Felice looks at Tommy. He looks back at her. "What are you looking at? Do you have a problem?" Felice shies away, "Oh, I'm sorry, I didn't mean to. I'm sorry! Thank you for the jacket!" Tommy turns away.

This is when the Officer is down to the last two names, and the last two are Felice Levito and Tommy Cade! In disbelief, Tommy and Felice look at each other like the blood has drained from their bodies. Felice, excited but puzzled, "Tommy?" Tommy is stunned, "Felice!!??" Felice puts her hand over her mouth, "Oh my God, it's you!" Tommy reacts quickly, grabbing Felice's arm and moving to the room's other side. Ashlie was confused. "Felice, where are you going?" Felice, still in shock, doesn't say a word to Ashlie. As Tommy and Felice sit there, Tommy puts his finger over her mouth. Again, He grabs her hand, and they quickly exit the Police station door.

Felice went back to the Present day for a moment.

"And that's how it all started again, right here in this Police department!"

SIX

True Love Never Dies

Felice and Tommy laugh as they run down the street, Tommy picks Felice up as high as he can, and they hug each other. Tommy goes to his knees. "I can't believe this! It's like a crazy dream!" For a moment, Tommy shows a vulnerable side to him. Felice puts her fingers through his hair, "I know!!" Tommy gets up. That was the worst day of my life when I moved away, but I always knew I'd see you again somewhere! The love is so strong between the two. They gaze into each other's eyes. Felice is about to cry. I can remember when you told me that! Tommy now regains his composure, putting his arm around her. "Let's go somewhere to talk." Tommy looks around to see if they are safe in rival gang territory, and they walk away.

SEVEN

Getting To Know One Another Again

Tommy and Felice are at a diner frequently occupied by E-6 Thunder; for the most part, they watch over it and its owners, a husband and wife, an elderly couple named Sammy and Ann. Several years back, a rival gang tried to take protection money from them and failed after Big Vic and E-6 Thunder ran them off. Tommy and Felice sit in the back of the Diner and talk. Felice sipping her drink, "See, that's why I had to leave my house. There was so much confusion there. It seemed as I was getting older, the more they argued, then I heard them talking about getting divorced. I didn't want to see or hear that. I know it's a common thing, but who wants to hear your parents talking about it, ya know? You remember your parents when you were a kid, thinking they were the happiest people on the planet, then one day, it's all gone. It was a shame all along. They were acting happy all those years because of me!! And then the guilt came. I don't know. So what happened to you?"

Tommy, with a look of frustration on his face, has a hard time opening up to anyone. He looks down at his plate, stammers a bit, "I don't even want to talk about it!" then slowly begins to open up, "Well, when they told me I was adopted, that started it all when I was "Eleven," that was real fucked up for me." "Especially when they told me my birth parents were dead, and then you are told they're alive and well, but you don't know where the hell they are." Tommy sits in a steady state and is angry. "I wish I could find them. I have a lot of shit to tell them!" Felice shakes her head, "What about Renee and Steve?"

Tommy, not comfortable at all, looks around to see if anyone is listening. "Renee always treats me like her son, but Steve's an asshole. He was

always flashing his money around, especially to Renee; he always put her down every chance he got. I don't know how many times she left him, then like a fool; she ran back because he begged her to come back after his boxing career was over. He was pissed off at the world, and when Renee wasn't around, he began to use me as a punching bag. Renee thought it would be a good idea for us to bond, so when he started to drive his trucks cross country, Renee wanted me to go with him, I begged and told her I didn't want to go, but she didn't listen!" Felice's jaw drops. "Are you serious? Why didn't you tell Renee what he was doing to you?"

Tommy gets very agitated, "Because I didn't want him to beat the shit out of her for defending me. Sometimes we would be gone for weeks at a time, and he'd fuckin' starve me and get a rise out of it! We'd go to diners, and he'd eat right in front of me." Once in a while, he would throw me a French fry or something and laugh and say, "Enjoy because that's your food for today!!" "That Fucker!" Felice brought to tears, "Oh Tommy, I'm so sorry!!" Tommy clenches his fist, "Yeah, I remember going home and eating everything I could get my hands on, but that wasn't the worst of it. Out of the torrid relationship that they had, they managed to have a daughter. Her name is Nicole. Steve was protective of her; as she grew, he began to look at me like he didn't trust me around her or something, so that was my cue to leave. That was six years ago, I decided to drop right here in the windy city!" Felice, still in tears, "Well, don't worry, Tommy, he can't hurt you anymore! I just feel so bad that you don't have any family." Tommy points his finger around him to his E-6 gang members, "See them. They're my family. They'll have my back to the end, no matter what!" Tommy sits back on the chair, becomes frustrated, and gets up. "Let's get out of here!" For a moment, Felice gazes back into the present at the Police station, very saddened, "I found it very amazing on Tommy's part that he told me and trusted me about his E-6 Thunder affiliation."

They were no regular bunch of thugs. Most of them, like Tommy, had jobs and watched and protected their streets against rapists, child abductors, abusers, thieves, and other slimes. Sometimes he told me that the ones that

did go astray were severely punished by the higher-ups. If you did go astray and did not follow the strict rules of their gang code, you were never seen or heard from again! This coming from one of the top men named Big Vic, whose own family was murdered by another rival street gang named "Crew Diablo" or "Diablo's Crew," who were so elusive they did not fly colors. They blended in with other street gangs and murdered them and their families, for the fun of it, and that's how E-6 started, and they vowed to watch each other's back and the innocent people in their community around them!

EIGHT

The Lighter Side

Two a.m. that same cold, dreary, damp night,

Tommy and Felice are still catching up. They sit on a park bench. Felice is still trying to console Tommy as she knows he has a lot of anger built up, but she is not pushing too hard, trying not to anger him further. Felice, looking down to the ground, "I can't believe Steve did that to you, Tommy! You know it's not your fault." Tommy sits with his chin on the fence, looking away from Felice. "Well, there are a lot of times I don't like to talk about it, ya know?" Turns to her, "Look, I'm not selfish or stupid. The world is a fucked-up place. I always tell myself there's always someone who has it worse than me." "I know that I don't know, but I always feel there's something I need to do, but I haven't found it yet!" Felice puts her hand on his shoulder, "Keep looking until you find it! Whatever it is, hey, who knows, maybe I could help you!" Tommy turns to her and smiles, "Yeah, If I'm lucky."

Tommy quickly changes the subject off of himself. "Hey, tell me, are you following anyone these days? Am I going to get beat up talking to you or something?" Felice laughs, "I'm not following anyone. I'm going with someone." Tommy laughs, "Look out now!" Tommy looks over his shoulder. "Now I know I'm in trouble!" They both start to laugh. Tommy has a hearty laugh and begins to nudge her a bit. "Well, tell me about this, dude?" Felice reluctantly replies, "I don't think you'd be interested." Tommy pokes her and laughs, "Come on, spill it out to me, man-tell me!" Felice turns her head away, "His name is Richie, and he's in college, and he's smart, and he has everything going for him, looks, money from his parents, and an attitude to match! After tonight he's lucky if I ever speak to him again! He thinks

his shit doesn't stink. God, I hate that about him! He thinks he owns me. Nobody owns me, anyway I think I'm going to break it off with him soon!" Tommy nods, "Way to go, Fe, don't make anyone take advantage of you whatever he did!" Tommy Laughs, "But it would be nice to have all that money he has. I'll visit you in your huge mansion one day, or maybe you could hire me as your pool boy or something."

Felice laughs, "Oh God, here we go; maybe I'd hire you as my pool boy in my own house with my money without Richie!" Tommy Laughs, "Now you're talkin. I like the thought of that!" Felice looks down at her watch that she has on a chain around her neck, "Oh man, Ashlie will kill me," Tommy looks down to the ground, "Why?" Felice was a bit nervous, "I don't know if anyone locked her door tonight when the party was broken up, and I told her I would be right home after we left the police station. She usually stays with her boyfriend. I have to go! Could you walk me?" Tommy, very laid back, "Sure! What are friends for? But I hope all 5-0 are gone!"Tommy and Felice begin to walk away from the bench and walk down the street where Ashlie's apartment is. Tommy continues to look over his shoulder because of rival gang members and the police. He walks with his shoulders slouched, "So what are you doing with your life, Fe? What do you want to do... in this stinking place we call life?" Felice thinks, "I'm in community college to become a Counselor, and I do a lot of artworks on downtime, and right now, I'm a waitress at some hole-in-the-wall diner!" Tommy nods his head, "Yeah, that's good. I want to become king and hang around for the rest of my life! You know, all females with big tits waving those things in my face all day and night!" Felice replies, "Oh yeah, and if you ever get married, I don't think your wife would appreciate that!" Tommy Laughs, "No, I don't think she'd go for that, Huh! She'll throw me out on my ear and take me for all my millions!" "Unless she's into that sort of thing," tries to get a rise out of Felice and does. Felice laughs, "You Asshole!" She hits him, and they crack up laughing.

NINE

The Lust

Felice and Tommy walk up the steps to Ashlie's apartment. Felice is reluctant to enter, so Tommy goes to the door first. The door is open slightly, and there are no lights on inside. Tommy, without hesitation, goes inside the apartment. Knowing Felice is on edge about going inside, he goes in to check it out. He puts on all the lights for her, looks in the closets and under the beds, locks all the windows for her, then walks out to the front doorway where Felice stands and says, "All clear for you inside, Fe!" The sexual tension builds between these two very fast. Tommy doesn't show it as much as Felice because of him being so nonchalant. Felice is trying to keep her emotions in check because, despite Richie's actions on this night, she doesn't want to betray him. Felice looks at Tommy as he passes her, and he walks to the other side, out the door. He leans against the doorframe in front of her. Felice stares at Tommy quite shy "Well, Tommy, I had a great night, but I have to go in." Tommy nods in agreement, "Yeah, I know." He looked at the ground nonchalantly. Felice, fearing she won't ever see him again, grabs his arms and says, "I want to see you tomorrow." Tommy nods his head and walks away. Felice stares at him as he walks away down the steps. Felice mesmerized him. She takes a deep breath...

TEN

The Blue-Collar Workers

Tommy works at a furniture warehouse and other E-6 gang members in the shipping area, but his true interest is screenwriting. He never shares this with anyone because he doesn't think anyone will listen. He always has a pen and pad ready in his back pocket in case he gets an idea. He mostly writes about his life experiences. As he loads the truck, he gets a good idea and begins to write. He leans on a piece of furniture to it. Tommy indulges in his writing and doesn't pay attention when the warehouse owner walks up. A co-worker of Tommy's taps his arm to let him know that the Boss is headed towards them.

The Boss catches Tommy and says, "very nasty, come on, Cade, let's get a move on, work, work, work! Stop playing around!" he walks past them, cursing him. Tommy looks up at his co-worker. "He's a fuckin" asshole! He needs to get a life for himself!" The co-worker laughs. Tommy's cell phone rings, and he answers, "Hello?" on the other end is Felice… "Tommy?" Tommy replies, "No, this is the king." Felice laughs, "Uh oh, here we go with this again!" Felice is at work in the kitchen. She goes into a corner, so the owner doesn't see her. Tommy grins, "What's up?" Felice talks softly, "Are you free for dinner tonight? I thought I would cook something for us!" Tommy, with no emotion, "Yeah, I don't care!" Felice seems confused by his answer, but she smiles, "Wow, you sure sound very enthusiastic about all this. What's wrong?" Tommy scratches his head. "Nothing. But what about the college boy?" Felice was getting risqué, "What about him? He's away. Like I said, He doesn't own me!" Tommy is secretly excited but doesn't show it, "Wow! She strikes again!" On the other end, Felice smiles, "So what is it, yes? Or no?" Tommy shakes his head. "What time?" Felice

waves to her waitress friend Cathy, giving her the thumbs-up sign. "How's seven?" Tommy nods his head. "Sounds good. I will be there!"

Tommy, with his quick decisions, hangs up the phone. Felice again is mesmerized by the aloof Tommy. Felice whispers to her co-worker, "He's unreal, Cathy." Cathy replies, "What's wrong?" "Wrong? There's nothing wrong here," Felice says. "It's just the way Tommy is. He's direct, but so unpredictable! He hasn't changed a bit! I can't stop thinking about him. Wait until you meet him, then maybe you will understand! I don't know what he has over me?" Cathy shakes her head. "Somebody's obsessed!" Felice smiles at her, and the cook rings the bell for their next orders.

ELEVEN

Stories from the E-6 crew

That same day, Six p.m.,

A few members of E-6 are hanging out at the diner. There's Rocco, Sal, nicknamed "Blondie" because of his unusually bright hair color, and The Greek, who are in a corner playing cards, wasting some time. At this moment, a young woman who is nineteen, very pretty. Her name is Denise, not wanting to become a statistic, is in her first year of college. However, she is still affiliated with the E-6 Thunder and other local girls. E-6 nicknamed her "Denny" from time to time. She has dated a few of the guys in the gang, but at one point, she stepped outside the box and fell in love with a Law student she had met during her classes. Denny comes storming into the diner while Rocco accuses Sal of hiding cards. Rocco shouts, "What the fuck, blondie? Take those fuckin cards out from under you. You're a cheating bastard!" Blondie laughs. "What did I do? You are paranoid." Rocco throws the cards at him, "When you're taking my money, I am paranoid?" as the two continue to bicker, Denny, very upset, walks up to the counter and asks Ann for water. Sal stops and looks and nudges The Greek's arm. The fellas all know that Greek has a thing for her. He says, "Take a lookie over there, Greek. It's your dream!" Rocco laughs, "Or your worst nightmare!" As Greek walks away, Sal whispers to Rocco, "but not soft enough for Denny not to hear." "Nothing special. I had her!" Denny turns around, "Yeah, Fuck you, Blondie! You couldn't handle all this, anyway!" Everyone around them laughs at Rocco through the rest of the cards he has in his hands at Sal and says, "Oooh, cut to size 'cuz' Denny on a roll." "I'm sorry, Sal, but there's nothing to cut, anyway." Flexing her pinkie... The crowd laughs. The Greek now walks up to Denny. The Greek leans on the counter, "Well, you won't have that problem with me!" Denny

looks at Greek. "What?" The Greek tries to cover it up, "Nothin. Where have you been? I haven't seen you that much!" Denny looks down at the counter. "Don't even ask," she thinks and then begins to open up. She sighs, "Ok, remember my fiancé, my Ex fiancé, Bobby?" The Greek nods his head, "Yeah, the Lawyer, dude?" Denny, "Yeah, that's him, well anyway, he turned out to be a complete scumbag! He told me out of the blue he couldn't get serious with anyone. He took a trip with his family, and about a month ago, it turns out he moved to Cali and was married to someone he worked with. I can give a shit about him, but it's just all the time wasted with him! What's wrong with me, Greek?" The Greek shakes his head, "C'mon, you didn't see that coming? Those kinds of guys are the worst! Turn around; let me see what you look like." Denny turns around for him. The Greek shrugs his shoulders, "Nothing wrong from the other end!" Denny smiles and hits his arm, "Stop you! but thanks anyway." The Greek pulls her close to him, "Hey listen, I'm never going to make the money that a lawyer makes, or anything fancy I'm a nine to fiver. You know, for a while now I was thinking about you and me getting together sometime? If you're interested?" Denny nods. "Yeah, maybe sometimes sounds like a plan."

Now Tommy walks through the front door and goes towards the back, sitting at the counter; almost immediately, his Ex-girlfriend comes running up to him; Tommy ignores her, turning around in his seat, just knowing she is going to start. Her name is Breanna, twenty-two, blonde hair, and big-chested. Tommy and Breanna have been a couple in the past and always had a stormy relationship after all the makeup and broke up, Tommy eventually grew tired of her and wanted to move on, but Breanna can't seem to let Tommy go even after Tommy told her repeatedly he wants no part of her. E-6 refers to her as "Tommy's stalker!" Sometimes, he uses Breanna for her money and sex! Sal laughs, "Uh Oh! Here she comes! Look out, Tommy! He's fuckin crazy. Look at the tits on her!" Rocco gets a charge out of all these laughs, "This is like a soap opera, my god!" Breanna pulled Tommy's arm, "Hi Tommy, how are you? I was looking all over for you!" Tommy smiles but turns away, "Yeah, hi." He

gets an idea and turns back to her, "I was short on my check this week. Do you have any money on you?" Breanna, without hesitation, "Sure, how much do you need?" Rocco laughs, listening to the conversation, "What a criminal!" Tommy gets up from his seat, very restless. "How much you got?" Breanna looks in her purse and pulls out money and shows it to him. "I have Ninety dollars on me, but I took a cab here to see you." He counts the money and gives her twenty back, taking seventy from her. Tommy is frustrated, "Thanks! Now you can get home. Now get the fuck out of here! You're an embarrassment." Breanna was stunned, "Tommy!" Tommy walks over to the soda case, gets a soda bottle, sits back down, and says to Breanna, "You still here? Didn't you hear me? Are you deaf?" Breanna, "But Tommy, let me explain!" Tommy shakes his head, "No, save it, Breanna. I know what your problem is. You're a fuckin whore!" Breanna starts to cry, "No, listen, Tommy, it's not like that at all." Tommy interrupts her, "No, you listen, babe, it's good to know if I ever need to get laid. I know where to go." Now he's making a complete fool of her, "Right?" Breanna cried, "No, Tommy, I love you!" He gets up, sliding the bottle of soda to her. "Oh, man! Get off my back, bitch!" Now he grabs her underneath her arm and starts looking out the door to her cab. Tommy very stern, "Is that your cab?" Breanna Cries, "Yes!" He walks her to the cab, opens the door, and throws her inside, shutting the door. Tommy to the cabbie, "Get her the hell home and away from me!" As the cabbie drives off, Breanna cries and shouts from the back seat, "Tommy, please don't do this to us! Please don't make me leave." Shouting, "Tommy! Tommy!" Patrons in the diner who see this take place all talk amongst one another. The Greek says, "That motherfucker is hardcore."

TWELVE

The First Date

Tommy catches a bus not far from where Felice lives and gets off after the next stop. Many people know who Tommy is, and they shout at him. Because he is wearing the colors of E-6, white and black, even people across the street shout, put their fists in the air, and chant, "E-6 Forever!!" An Elderly lady even stops him and says, "It's because of you and your friends we can walk safely around here again!" She hugs Tommy, and he nods and says, "Thank you!!" Tommy looks down at the money he took from Breanna, walks into a florist, buys one red rose wrapped in nice paper, and then goes into a nearby liquor store to buy a bottle of red and white wine. Now Tommy walks out of the liquor store, and there's a bum lying up against the wall. Tommy takes out a twenty-dollar bill and shoves it into the bum's pocket as he sleeps. A few steps down is Ashlie's apartment. He walks in, rings the bell, and Felice buzzes him in. He passes people on the stairwell. They all know, again by the colors he wears, that he is an E-6 Thunder gang member, a young boy no more than the age of 9 walking down the steps with his mother and saying to his mom, "Look, mom, he's from E-6 they are the baddest!" the boy's mom replies, "I'm sorry!" clutching onto her son as she walks by Tommy fearing how he would react! Tommy smiles, "Don't worry, Mrs., we're the good guys!" The boy's mother nods with a smile but is still leery of him. The boy asks Tommy for an autograph. Like a local celebrity, Tommy signs a piece of paper the young boy handed him and hands it back. The boy says he wants to grow up and be just like him. Tommy says, "Thanks," but urges the boy to stay in school, and he walks to Felice's door. Tommy knocks on the door, leaning on the frame. Felice opens the door and has a big smile on her face, very excited to see him. "Tommy! How are you? Come in." He enters the apartment. "Hey Fe, how are you?" Being

the complete gentleman that he is, he handed her the rose. "Oh, this is for you." Felice takes the rose and looks at Tommy with a smile. "Oh, thank you. That's so sweet of you, thanks!" Tommy puts the two bottles of wine on the table. And he begins to look around the apartment. "So this is what this apartment looks like with all the lights on, huh?" Felice nods and looks around. "Yeah, what do you think?" Tommy continues to look around. "Nice. So, where's your roomie?" Felice, "Oh, she went out for a while. She'll be back later." He turns towards her. "What did you cook for dinner?" Felice walks to the kitchen. "I hope you like spaghetti?" Tommy very nonchalantly nods, "Yeah, that's cool." Again, the extreme sexual tension between them. They just look at one another. Felice is quite nervous, but happy. "Well, would you like to sit down? Over here." Tommy, "Yeah, I don't care." They both sit down and look at each other. "Wow, I can't believe it, Fe. You haven't changed a bit." Felice looks into his eyes, "You too. You look great!" Tommy, having the utmost respect for Felice, knows where this can easily go. He doesn't want to ruin what they have together, so he changes the subject. "So the other night, you told me you were going to school for counseling?" Felice looks down, "Yeah, and art, but I think I have to take a few semesters off. I just can't pay for it right now. It pisses me off because I wanted to help troubled kids for the counseling part and then bring my art into it to work in a school or something, but paying the bills comes first." Tommy nods, "Yeah, life does this shit to us. Sometimes you feel it chews you up and spits you out, looking away, and then we're here to figure all this shit out ourselves! But I guess you need a diploma to counsel someone, right? But for your art, all you need is your imagination. It can take you places if you're talented enough."

There are two beer glasses on the table. Tommy opens the red bottle of wine and pours it into both glasses. "Hey, this is the first time I've ever had wine in a beer glass!" They both laugh. Felice puts her hand on her forehead. "Oh, I'm so sorry about that. Me and Ashlie are so unorganized sometimes. Let me go check the spaghetti." Felice gets up and goes into the kitchen. As she does, Tommy gets up and looks around. Tommy is

still drinking his wine, "So Felice do you have any artwork of yours you can show me?" Felice concentrated for the moment on her cooking abilities from the kitchen, "Oh, in the bedroom." Tommy makes his way to the bedroom. In a nice way, Felice tries to stop him and puts down the pots and pans and runs into the bedroom, "Please, Tommy, it's not very good." Tommy stops and stares at her, "how is anyone going to judge your work if you don't let anyone look at it?" Felice pulling his arm, "Tommy, No!" Tommy, very uncommunicative, goes into the bedroom and looks around, "Where is it?" he goes under a bed that is hers, pulls out a drop cloth and unwraps it containing Felice's artwork, and looks at the pictures. "These are really nice, Fe!" Felice looks at them as well. "Do you think so?" Tommy nods. "Shit, yeah! Can you take some criticism, though?" Felice, "Yeah, spit it out!" Tommy points to the picture, "I can see you only put two colors in the sky where you should have had many different colors. That would make this picture pop out at you, but I can see your imagination is unlimited. You have tons of talent. I can see that there is no bull!" Felice smiles. "Really? How do you know so much about art?" Tommy continues to study the pictures. "Well, I like art too! I like to create. It keeps me in check. One day, though, I would like to write a screenplay or something for the movies!" Felice, "Wow! That's great, Tommy!" Felice looks down at her pictures. "Yeah, well, I wish others were as enthusiastic about my art as you are. Richie told me to stick with counseling because he felt I don't have any talent at all in art!"

Tommy looks at her. "Does Richie wear glasses?" Felice replies, "No?" Tommy replies, "Well, maybe you should invest in a pair for him!" The two begin to laugh and drop on the bed together. Now Felice remembers that the food is still cooking on the stove, "Oh my god, the food is done!" She pulls Tommy's arm and sits him on the floor, where she has a blanket set up, and serves him his food. Felice sits on the other side of him, and they begin to eat. They stare at one another. Again, Tommy doesn't want to ruin anything when Felice starts to talk, "So tell me about your friend Ashlie?" Felice is drinking her wine, "Well, she is really smart. She's going to become a clothes designer. She's going to school for it. She'll be done

with it soon." Tommy gets restless, "Hey, Fe, let's get out of here and go somewhere!" Tommy quickly grabs Felice's hand as they laugh and run out the door.

Now for a moment, Felice breaks in, and it is back to the present; tears stream down her face as rain pours outside, beating on the window in pain. Felice, looking out the window, "We could have done anything together. It was like we had been together all those years. Nothing had changed between us. She shakes her head; Tommy was always sporadic like that, always! Also, everyone knew who he was. For someone who was deemed as somewhat of a thug, he was the kindest person! I saw him give money to bums on the street and kids who knew him and looked up to him. He told them to stay in school and don't follow his path." Laughing and thinking, "He once even helped an old lady cross the street." "I saw him do that once," Laughing. "He called himself a Boy Scout!"

THIRTEEN

Tommy's Flip Side

Tommy takes Felice to a small park in E-6 territory. It is nicely lit, and the night is beautiful. As they walk, they begin to reminisce and go over old times when they were young. Tommy walked with his hands in his pockets, scraping his feet, and looking down to the ground. They stop at the swings. Felice sits in one, and Tommy sits in the other. Tommy looks at Felice. "Hey Fe, remember when we were young? We never got along." Felice smiles, "You can say that again. We never got along for anything." Tommy wipes his nose with his hand, "I used to lose because you always went crying to Renee... She beat my ass." Felice laughed, "Yeah, I remember that! Tommy, I think, in a psychological way, you were worse than I was. You were a mad genius or something? You manipulator!" They laugh.

Then Tommy starts to think. He takes out a small bottle of vodka from his jacket pocket. "You know Felice, I wish I could find my birth mother just to tell the bitch what I really think of her. You know, as I said, I always thought of Renee as my mother, but it's just not the same. I've got to find her, just to talk." Felice, upbeat for Tommy's sake, "I have a good idea, my laptop crashed, but tomorrow when I go to school, I can check it out on one of the computers. We can search for her if you have her name and where she might live. I will try to help you." Tommy, very confused, finishes and throws the empty bottle of vodka down to the ground, shrugs his shoulders, "Come on."

Part Two

Felice and Tommy catch a cab into Downtown Chicago. They walk the streets laughing and looking into store windows. Felice looks at one in particular, a high-end department store. Tommy takes notice. There is a shirt and shoes that Felice would like, but it is too much for her to afford. Tommy walks close to her and also looks into the window with her. Tommy smiles, "Ahh, you found something you like, huh? Come on, let's go in." Felice shakes her head, "I can't afford anything in here." Tommy pulls her arm into the store. When they go in, they look around the store in amazement. A saleswoman walks up to them, "Can I help you?" Tommy, very laid back, "Yeah, uh, could you please show this lovely young lady some new clothes? And how good she looks, I think, in size zero!" The saleswoman smiles, "Sure." Felice laughs, "But Tommy!?" Tommy nonchalantly doesn't worry, turns to the saleswoman, and shows her some things. When nobody is looking, Tommy looks up to see if there are any cameras and starts to put clothes in his jacket for Felice.

Almost an hour passes, and they are still in the store. Tommy sits in a chair while Felice and the saleswoman return. Tommy gets up, saleswoman to Felice, "Will that be all?" Felice turns to Tommy, "Tommy, don't you want anything for yourself?" Tommy smiles, "I can't get anything. You spent all my money on you!" Felice nods her head and laughs. Tommy hands the saleswoman the money when she turns away, Tommy looks up at the camera and shows Felice the things that he stole, and he says, "No, I have all the things I want!" Felice's eyes open wide, "Tommy, are you crazy?" Tommy says, "Yeah!" Felice replies, "The cameras!"

The saleswoman turns back to them and hands them the bag. Tommy takes it and taps Felice's arm. "Bet you can't beat me out that door?" He takes off for the door. Felice laughs very hard and runs after him. The saleswoman, quite confused, shouts to them, "Wait, you forgot your change and receipt!" As they both run out the door, people look at them. They run down the street and stop to catch their breath. They Laugh, Felice

out of breath, "Well, that's the last time we can go into that store." Walking alongside him, Tommy hands her the bag, stuffing the items he stole. Felice laughs, "I can't believe you." Looking inside the bag, Tommy walks with his hands in his pockets, "What?" Felice, amazed, "How could you do that? Walk into a store and just take everything in sight!" Tommy shrugs his shoulders, "Hey, when you don't have a lot, you gotta do what you gotta do to stay alive, whether or not it's for food or clothes, whatever!" he grabs the bag nonchalantly turning away from her, "Oh you don't want it? Ok, let's take it back!" They laugh so hard again as Tommy plays cat and mouse with her. Tommy, very shrewd, lets her try and catch the bag, but she fails to do so. "Come on, Fe. Do you want it here?" He acts like he's going to give into her but immediately takes it back, "No, you don't!"

This goes on for a while. Suddenly, Tommy drops the bag and grabs her. They both stop laughing and just stare at each other. Felice almost looks breathless at this time. Tommy kisses her on the mouth. She starts to think back to when they were children at the going away party, for Tommy and his family. They were both in the basement at her house when Tommy kissed her. Felice, at this time, is having a hard time to stop herself. Out of breath, she begs Tommy to stop because of the impending relationship she has with her boyfriend. Felice, out of breath, almost in tears, "No, Tommy, please. I really want to, but Richie?!" Tommy is still very nonchalant about the whole thing about Richie, "Oh yeah, collage boy. I keep forgetting. He looks around. Let's get out of here." Tommy walks away. Felice, stunned, rubs her forehead and then follows him. For a moment, Felice back into the present at the police department, still looking out the window, "See what I'm saying?" Tommy could then change his whole perspective on himself and be somewhat of a bad boy!

FOURTEEN

Doing the right thing

The time is three-thirty a.m. at Ashlie's apartment,

Felice and Ashlie are up talking. They both are dressed in very sexy lingerie. Felice begins to talk about Tommy. Felice sits on the edge of her bed, "Ash, I don't know what to do." Ashlie sitting in a chair, eating Ice cream out of a carton, "What do you mean? About what?" Felice, confused, "You know, this thing about Tommy! I mean, Richie will be back by the weekend." Ashlie drops the carton of Ice cream on her nightstand, "Hey listen, Fe, Tommy is a real hottie and all. He's really good-looking and all, but do you really want to get involved with a gangbanger? Is that the direction you want to go in your life?" Felice looks out, "But you don't know him. He's really talented. Underneath all of that anger, he has something I need to find out, and just what I've been telling you about him isn't enough!" Ashlie shakes her head, "Ooh God! I know where this is going!" Felice wakes up, "You have a guy whose name is Richie remember? Mr. College slash rich boy, slash going somewhere in his life! Means you'd be set for life!"

Felice looks at Ashlie, "Don't you see Ashlie? I don't want my whole life to revolve around money! It's not about money at all, not what I'm talking about, anyway. I'm talking about love, Ashlie really loving someone. You know as well as I do Richie is a complete asshole to me. He's always gone, never tells me where he's going, and when he is around, he's always so concentrated on himself! Don't get me wrong. I know it sounds like I have a schoolgirl crush or something. And I am not trying to get back at Richie because of what he does to me. I know sometimes I sound a little naïve, but I'm not! Trust me. But when I saw Tommy again, the way I feel

for him, nothing could take that feeling away. Tommy is the real deal!" Ashlie moves closer to Felice seriously. "Does he feel the same for you?" Felice nods her head, "Ooh yeah, I know so! We would have gone at it tonight if I hadn't stopped it. I want to break it off with Richie first!" Ashlie, "Ooh, my dear Felice, you are too good." Laughs, "Why don't you have both of them, Good vs. Evil!" Felice shakes her head, "You know me better than that. I don't want to make the same mistakes my parents made and regret it for the rest of my life! There's too much of that going on in the world like today. People have no morals anymore!" Ashlie smiles. "You know Felice, you sound like a nun!" The two girls burst out laughing. Ashlie gets on Felice's bed, "So, sister Felice, tell me more about this mystery man, Tommy." Still laughing, then Felice gets more serious. "He's everything. Like I told you, we grew up together. We were best friends when we were young, before he moved away. It's funny because before he moved away, he told me that we were going to see each other again somewhere, someday, but when you're a kid, you try your hardest to believe it.

Anyway, one minute, he could be doing one thing, and the next, he could be doing something totally different. You would have to get to know him well before understanding him." "I'm telling you," she smiles, "he's so unpredictable but so dependable!" Ashlie gets up, "Well, Fe, you have to do what's best for you. Nobody can tell you what to do." Ashlie begins to walk out of the bedroom. Felice Says, "Where are you going, Ash?" Ashlie replies, "To get my phone, all of this talk about guys, it's making me horny!" Felice laughs and then puts her head down on her pillow.

Part Two

The very next morning, the sun shines brightly through the window, and Felice's cell phone rings. It's six a.m. She answers the phone. Felice moves the hair out of her eyes, "Hello?" It's Richie on the other end. Felice, not too enthusiastic at all to hear from him, "Oh yeah, hi Richie. Oh no, I have to get ready for work." She looks at her clock. "Shit, I overslept. Listen, can I call you later? I have to talk to you

about something really important." On the other end, Richie tries to interrupt her, but she talks over him, "No, no, I have to go. I'll call you later. Bye!" She hangs up the phone and shakes her head. "Phew!"

FIFTEEN

Meeting the family

Felice is at the end of her shift at the diner she works in downtown. It is the dinner rush and is a very hectic time. As she continues to take people's orders, she looks at the clock. She has about five minutes left before she can leave. She takes down orders as people keep calling out to her, and it is common for men to hit on her. She is waiting on a group of businessmen. One in particular, a very handsome guy, orders, "Yeah, could I have today's special... and your phone number?" Felice looks down at his ring finger and notices he's married. She walks away, shaking her head in dismay, to herself, "Oh, please! Go home to your wife!" The men laugh. Felice walks back to the cooking area and puts the order in, takes off her apron, and walks up to her Boss, who is counting today's profits at his desk, Felice takes out the money she has earned for the diner, and Stan takes what he owes her in tips, Felice reaches out and takes the money and says, "Stan I'm out of here right now, ok?" Stan counting his money, "Sure Felice, you can go but be back here at six tomorrow till close, we're short, and I'll need you till closing!" Felice puts on her jacket, "Wow, long day tomorrow, but I'll be here at Six a.m., See ya!" Felice exits the diner.

Moments later, Felice walks down the street and reaches for her cell phone to call Tommy. Dialing his number, he waits a moment, then Tommy picks up, "Hello?" Felice is very excited, "Tommy, hi, it's Felice. I'm sorry to bother you. I know you're at work and all." Tommy is very sullen, "No, I'm not working. I'm on vacation!" Felice laughs, Tommy smiles, leaning against a wall, "No, that's o.k. What's up?" Felice stops, "I wanted to see you later. I really want to talk to you some more if that's alright." Tommy pauses and then stammers, "Yeah, I think we can do that. I get out of here around five. Meet me at Artie's diner around Five thirty. I have some

things to take care of first, o.k.?" Felice was almost lost for words but not showing it, "ok, I'll see you at five-thirty then." Tommy nonchalantly "ok." and he hangs up the phone. Felice, still on the phone, excited, "Bye!"

Felice breaks into the present a moment at the Police station,

"See, everyone, including my friends, thought I was crazy and a very insecure person, but that's not true. Like I said, I've always been able to stand on my own two feet and take care of things myself. But again, when I was around Tommy, it was like I was totally into him. It really scared me. Just thinking about him right now makes me lose all control of everything. You know, I knew a lot of people back then, but no one will ever have the same impact that he had on me. No one! It was just the way he did things... So anyway, later that night..."

Five thirty that same evening, in front of Artie's diner, Felice pulls up in a cab on the opposite side of the street. She pays the driver and notices a commotion in front of Artie's, the cabbie drives away Felice backs off for a moment to see what is going on, and it is no other than Tommy and another E-6 member named Aaron, Tommy's ex Breanna, and this time her friend Lisa, Breanna is in a somewhat drunken rage, yelling and screaming. Felice watches from across the street. Tommy yelling at Breanna and grabs her underneath her arm. "Am I gonna have to tell you again? Stop coming around here. If I want you, I'll call you." he turns to Lisa, and Lisa gets a cab. Lisa grabs Breanna, "Tommy. I told her not to come down here, but she wouldn't listen. You have some kind of hold on her. "Come on, Breanna!" And again, Breanna screams and cries, "I love you, Tommy! I will be there any time for you! Please let me make it up to you! Please!" A cab pulls up, and people on the street, including Felice, witness this happening.

Tommy was furious, "Get this stalker in the fuckin" cab. This is an everyday thing now?" Aaron opens the cab door and literally throws Breanna inside of it. Lisa follows her inside, Tommy walks up to the driver's window

and gives him money as Breanna continues to scream, "Tommy, I love you!" Tommy looks in the back of the cab, pointing his finger at her, "Hey Breanna, It's over between us once and for all. I don't want it anymore!" As Breanna continues to carry on, the cabbie begins to get mad, "Hey buddy, no disrespect, man, but I don't need this shit. Come on!" Tommy takes a couple of extra dollars and hands it to him, "Here, take her where they need to go, ok?" The cabby takes the money. As Breanna shouts, she raises her foot and SMASHES her foot with her high heels right through the back window. Glass flies everywhere as Breanna screams.

The cabby curses as he drives off, Breanna in a drunken rage, "I don't know what I ever did wrong to you, Tommy, but I'll never give up on you. Your Mine!!" Aaron to Tommy as they watch the cab drive off, "That bitch is a serious stalker. She is fucking crazy! Well, I guess that's how they act when you give them a good fuck now and then!" They laugh, and Tommy scratches his head. "Yeah, tell me about it." As they walk up to the sidewalk, people are staring at them. Tommy looks up and says to everyone looking, "Show's over, curtains down. Everyone can go home now."

Everyone starts to walk away except Felice, who walks over to them from across the street. She smiles, and Tommy and Felice look at one another. Felice walks over to them, her hands in her pockets, "Wow, that was some show. That was better than some movies I've seen lately." Tommy looks up at her, quite stunned that she was there. "Oh, Fe, I didn't notice you were standing there. How much of that did you see?" Felice replies, "Enough!" Tommy looks around, "Well, I'm sorry you had to see that." Felice smiles, "So that was the important thing you had to do?" Tommy walked with his hands in his pockets, "No, that was a pain in my ass!"

The three walk into the diner. Tommy holds the door open for Felice and scratches his head, "Oh, Aaron, this is my friend Felice, I told you about." "Felice this is Aaron," Felice nods, "Hello." Aaron replies, "What's going on!" Tommy holding the interior door as Felice and Aaron walk in, "Come on in, Fe, I'll introduce you to some of the guys." As they walk in, there are about

fifteen E-6 Thunder gang members there playing cards, others sitting and talking. Aaron walks away, talking to some of the crew members. Both heads of the E-6 are there. The two brothers, Big Vic and his brother named Simon Gatchie, are talking business in the corner of the diner. As Tommy and Felice walk in the back, the diner's owner comes out from the back, "Tommy, Tommy, what are you doing out there? You guys are supposed to be protecting the neighborhood, not trashing it. Especially in front of my store." Tommy shrugs his shoulders, "What do you want, Sammy, she's a psycho!" Sammy's wife, Ann, comes out from the back, "Ooh, back off, Sam. Tommy can't help it if he's that handsome and the girls love him!" E-6 gang members laugh, Felice smiles, and Tommy shouts and laughs, "You tell him to me, Annie! Thanks!" Sal blondie shout, "Wherever Tommy goes, he creates havoc!" Tommy smiles, "Sit down, Blondie!" Tommy hugs Felice and shouts to them, "Everyone, this is my friend Felice, and Felice, this is my family!" Felice nods and smiles quite shy as Tommy walks her through the guys, "Hello!" Many of them say to her as they walk through, "What the hell are you doing with him? He's no good. Come with me." Tommy laughs, "Too late, she's with me!" The guys go back to what they were doing. Tommy continues to hug Felice as he walks with her, "Let's go sit in the back at a booth!" They sit in a secluded booth all the way back of the diner. Tommy sits on the opposite side of the booth facing Felice. He slouches in the seat with one foot up on it.

Felice looks at E-6 and smiles, "You sure have a lot of friends!" Tommy shakes his head, "This is nothing, you're in the inner circle. E-6 is all around Chicago... A couple hundred of us, at least. There's a lot, I don't know." Felice was very interested, "Wow!" Tommy whispers to her, "Do you see those two big dudes over there?" Tommy, referring to Big Vic and his brother Simon Gatchie, "They run this whole thing. They are brothers. Their entire family was murdered about ten years ago. Their parents owned an Italian restaurant in the next town over, when three armed mother fuckers came in when they were closing up, they took their father in the back room and beat the shit out of him while the other two beat and raped their mother and sister and made their father watch. After they

tortured them for hours, they shot all three execution styles, then hung the bodies in the basement and stripped them of their clothes. They put a nail into their father's head with a note attached saying, "This is what happens when you don't pay up!"

Felice looks at the Gatchie brothers, "Oh my God! How horrible! What did the police say?" Tommy replies, "Huh, what police? There was a little search, but after a while, the police stopped looking, and then it just died out. The Gatchie brothers were young then, but now look at them!" Felice shakes her head, "They are huge guys!" Tommy looks at them, "They work out like crazy, swearing redemption for their parents. They think it was a gang forcing their parents into giving them protection money and their father missing some payments, and they did them in! Anyway, Simon is really fucked up! I have seen him take out three dudes at once. If you talk to him, don't look him in the eyes, and he hates his name, Simon. That's why we call him Gatch!" Felice knows this really bothers Tommy, and she grabs his hands, "That's unimaginable!" Tommy, looking out, starts to stammer, "Yeah, sometimes I say to myself, what's this all about? There's got to be something more, you know? I always want to know what's the purpose?" Felice is very caring, "I'd like to help you find it, Tommy. I want to be with you!"

Tommy looks over to Big Vic's table, where he sees E-6 member Rocco talking to Big Vic, and now Rocco is walking over to him. Tommy whispers to Felice, "Something's going down!" Felice is a bit nervous, "What?" Tommy puts his finger over his mouth, "Sh, sh, sh," Rocco walks over to their table, "I'm sorry to bother both of you, but Tommy, Big Vic wants to see you!" He whispers in Tommy's ear, and Tommy nods his head. Rocco begins to walk away, Tommy to Felice close to her ear, "stay here I'll be right back!" Felice nods and watches Tommy walk up to and sit down at Big Vic's table, and she looks as she sees what happened to her childhood friend and knows for sure she needs to and wants to help him, in any way possible, she stares from a distance.

Now at Big Vic and Gatchie's table... Big Vic, counting money, "Hey Tommy, I'm sorry to bother you and your girl over there, but I have a little something I need you to take care of over the weekend." Tommy nods, "Yeah, anything. What is it?" Big Vic talks very low, "Let me tell you the story first, my cousin, who's divorced, moved to the south side in an apartment building with her two young daughters. She doesn't have a lot of money, and she had to move into this shithole, anyway, there is this mother fucker who lives in this building, a real fuckin scumbag. He goes by the name of Sassy, and his rap sheet is longer than my arm. He was convicted many times of rape and child molestation. You name it, he did it. He comes out of the can for a while, lays low, then gets his victims. He is starting to harass my cousin now and her thirteen-year-old daughter. She says he won't leave her alone. He follows the kid to school. When she comes out, he's waiting for her, the whole fuckin building is terrified of him, and I'm worried about my cousins." Tommy looks at Big Vic, "Say no more, anything you need me to do here, I'll do! But what about 5-0?" Big Vic and Gatch laugh, "Cops? What about them? They'll be eating doughnuts and sucking their mistresses' titties!" The three laugh. Gatch looks at Big Vic But tells him about the problem.

Big Vic nods his head and brings Tommy closer to him, "The problem..., Word is he's connected with crew Diablo! He's a low ranker," Gatch jumps in, "We don't want the whole Diablo crew to come down on us, though!" Tommy nods his head, "Big Vic, I want my best to do this, You, Aaron, Rocco, The Greek, Sal Blondie, Me, and Gatchie! and don't worry, you guys will get paid for this." Tommy shakes his head, "Hey, I can speak for me and the rest of the guys, don't worry, we'll do it for nothing!! Just to get that fucker off the street is a good thing. Anyway, it will send a message across Chi-town we don't play!"

Felice watches from a distance in the booth, Big Vic and Tommy get up and hug one another, "And don't worry about the people in the building. They'll be glad to get rid of this fucker! Trust me!" Big Vic pulls Tommy close, "Saturday Eleven p.m." Tommy nods, "Talk to you later!" Tommy

walks away back to Felice. She knows just by the look on Tommy's face that something important was said, but when he reaches the table, she doesn't say a word... "Fe, I'm sorry. I gotta take you home! We will pick this up tomorrow, ok?" Felice gets up out of the booth, "Sure!" Tommy lightens up a bit, "I will walk you home, my lady!" Felice smiles, and they walk out the diner doors.

The Walk Home

There is a light mist outside as Tommy and Felice walk down the street. Tommy reaches into his pocket and takes out a pint of vodka, and takes a swig. Felice looks at him, "Tommy, do you have a place to stay?" Tommy looks up, "What do you mean? A place to crash?" Felice replies, "Yeah. Where are you staying?" Tommy, with a rebellious manner, "Well, let me check my calendar here. Sunday and Monday, I slept on the street. Tuesday, I slept where I work. Last night, I crashed into some young lady's house. I can't remember her name, though. Oh, but that doesn't count. We didn't really sleep, forget about that!" Felice, with a slight smile, "Um, I don't want to know about that one." Tommy smiles, "No? It won't be hard to explain." Felice grabs his arm, a little despondent about what Tommy just said, but smiles anyway, "No, thank you, you could keep that adventure to yourself." Tommy laughs, "Hey, I have a good idea." Tommy takes another swig of vodka, "What?" Felice replies, "How about staying with me so I could keep you out of trouble for a while, and we can talk about old times day and night? I'm sure Ashlie wouldn't mind that she's hardly there, anyway. What do you say?" Felice, hoping he says the right thing. Tommy looks at her, "I'll give you some money for rent, ok? It'll keep me off the frigging street!" They walk away.

SIXTEEN

Redemption for the innocent

Saturday Ten forty-five p.m., Fifteen minutes before go-time,

The E-6 gang members pull up, all wearing their colors, in Sal Blondie's van across the street from the apartment building in which the multiple convicts named Sassy is terrorizing, E-6 getting ready... Big Vic is in the passenger's seat, "I want this mother fucker dead! But I want to torture him first. I found out the cops aren't even bothering him anymore because he is a low ranker in Diablo's crew. They're paying the crooked cops to look away from him, 5-0 now consider him a section 8, and this is the only place he can live, and 5-0 can give a shit about the people who live here in the building, giving him power and free reign over everything in there." Very direct to his guys, "after we kill him I want his hands chopped off that will teach these fuckers not fuck with kids!" E-6, without saying a word, nod their heads. Gatch pulls out his gun and a rope, Tommy conceals a butcher's knife, while the others have assorted weapons and tags around the place. "If 5-0 or Diablo's crew gets involved, I'll take the rap. I'm a marked man, anyway!" The clock hits Eleven, "Let's go!" They get out of the car and walk across the street to the building on this dark and misty night. Big Vic turns to his guys, "Listen, I don't know what we're going to confront in there! Stay close." They descend up to the building and walk into the dreary lobby. Loud music comes out of a top-floor apartment. People come out of their rooms frightened, Tommy and Gatch quietly shake their heads, telling them to go back into their apartments and close their doors. Everyone knows who they are there for, the infamous Sassy. Who has the building's residents on total lockdown, people cry with joy as E-6 thunder walks past them. Now as they approach the apartment door, shouts and moans sound out over loud music. Sassy shouts, "That's it

bitch, suck my mother fuckin dick ooh yeah..." Sassy, not knowing at this time his minutes, are numbered at the hands of E-6. The insane Sassy says to his victim, "On the other side of the door, I own this world. You are a sweet thing now, aren't you?" Now at this time, a girl cries and screams as she is being raped. Out in the hallway, Big Vic gives the signal to Rocco and Aaron, and they kick the door in. Once inside, the E-6 Thunder rushes in the door, orgy's takes place with a lot of Sassy's men taking advantage of many young girls. The apartment has many rooms, and the girls scream and scatter. Tommy grabs one of the men and holds the butcher's knife up to his neck, and shouts, "Are you Sassy?" The guy was very shaken. "No, no, I'm not!" Tommy shouts, "You fuckin scumbag!" Throws the guy against the wall and stabs him, blood flies everywhere. Gatch picks up another guy and throws him on a coffee table, and he crashes through it. The music blares as E-6 members take as many of the young girls as they can out of the apartment to safety, fights begin to pursue as the guys in the apartment begin to fight back. Big Vic throws one guy out the window as they make their way to the back of the apartment, and shouts, as he holds another guy by his neck, "Where the fuck is Sassy?" The guy replies, In the back room, "he's back there!" Big Vic grabs the guy by his testicles and squeezes them. The guy lets out a horrific scream, Big Vic takes out a gun and shoots him in the head, and Sal Blondie gets attacked by three guys at once and gets stabbed in his arm. Tommy, Rocco, and Aaron begin to wrestle them off Sal Blonde.

The guys see that E-6 have the upper hand and begin to flee the apartment. Tommy and Aaron take out pistols and begin shooting them in the hallway, not giving them time to escape. Bodies drop everywhere. People peek out their doors, Tommy shouts, "Get back in your fuckin apartments and don't come out till we are gone, damn it!" They shut their doors, Tommy and Aaron run back into the apartment, where Big Vic and the rest of E-6 are. Aaron begins to tag the walls, Gatch and Big Vic kick in the door where they believe Sassy is, and they break the door down, once inside the room is dark, and the young girl whimpers in the corner, her arms are chained to the wall she is completely nude, "Please don't hurt me!?"

Big Vic looks with anger and disgust. Big Vic replies, "We're not here to hurt you. We are here to get you out of here!" Rocco and Gatch break the chains off her and cover her up. The young girl cries as they take her out of the room, "Thank you!" Big Vic shouts to Sassy, "Come out, you fuck, you pussy! Time to pay the piper!" Tommy begins to trash the room with a bat, Sassy peeks out and is hiding in a closet in the room, and charges out of the closet with a machete-wielding it and almost hits Big Vic, and Tommy comes up from behind him and cracks him in the head, with the bat Sassy now drops the machete, but is not knocked out because he's very high he drops to his knees and laughs, and spits at Big Vic, "You fuckin assholes don't know who you're dealing with." Big Vic spits back at him, "You piece of shit, I don't give a fuck who we're dealing with, pick this fucker up and bring him over to that desk!" Gatch and Tommy bring Sassy over to a desk in the corner of the room. Rocco shouts, "We're E-6 Thunder, motherfucker!" Sassy laughs as they drag him to the desk and replies, "E-6 Pussies!" Tommy and Gatch hold Sassy stretching his penis on the table. Now Big Vic takes a knife, stabs, and pins Sassy's penis to the desk. Now he begins to beg for mercy in unbelievable pain. Gatch shouts like a crazy man in Sassy's ear, "Do you like that mother fucker!! That will teach you not to fuck with kids!" Big Vic shouts to Tommy and Gatch, "Put his fuckin' hands out!" Tommy and Gatch pin both of Sassy's hands on the table. Aaron hands him the machete that Sassy had and chops both of his hands off, blood spies everywhere. Sassy screams in horror, then goes into shock and drops onto the desk. Big Vic, enraged, without fear, shouts in Sassy's ear, "You cocksucker. Tell the devil E-6 sent you!" he takes out a knife and stabs him in his skull, finally killing him. Big Vic takes off out the room, the rest of the guys follow him except Aaron, who continues to tag the room, then tags Sassy's battered and lifeless body with the E-6 Thunder logo, then he runs out the room, out to the hallway, walking passed the dead bodies in which Tommy and he killed earlier, the tenants in the building know it's over, and begin to come out of their apartments, and begin to clap, and make the sign of the cross and thank them, as they pass walk down the steps Big Vic is stopped by his cousin she has tears in her eyes, Big Vic looks at her, "Call 911' It's

over!" and he walks out the door, walks across the street and into the car, and they drive off.

Part Two

Felice, back to the present, it all started from there. E-6 Thunder made headlines. Felice reaches into her bag and pulls out the first front-page news article that E-6 made for their heroic efforts for the innocents. Felice opens it up and hands it to the police sergeant. These were real heroes in my book! The police Sergeant looks at it and hands it back to Felice, "I remember this!" But before the newspaper articles, Tommy was very secretive about everything that E-6 was doing, but I found out but didn't say anything. He didn't want to put innocent people around him in danger. But it wouldn't be long before their acts spread around the country. But Big Vic and Gatch had bigger plans. They wanted to start vigilante factions in New York and California enforced with their strict rules! The Police Sergeant looks away. After the Sassy incident, our Chief Officer informed us not to touch E-6 for the slaying, to cover it up, because our hands were tied with Sassy. Before he was murdered, he was running around the streets terrorizing everyone (looking away, being a real person for a moment).

Because he was section eight, we couldn't do anything about him, and more so because he was associated with Diablo's crew. The Police department turned the other way at that time because we felt Diablo's crew would start a war in the streets. There were so many of them, we were looking out for the citizens that Chief resigned after that massacre. He told us to sweep the whole Sassy thing under the rug and not to touch E-6, noted they don't harm any innocent people. The Department figured if Diablo's crew had a problem with the killing of Sassy, and if E-6 had claimed it, they would fight it out amongst themselves and leave the Police department and, most of all, innocent people out of it! But no matter what you say, Felice, they still were against the law! Felice cries and becomes angry, "Hey they weren't choirboys, but let me ask you a question, do you

get paid for doing your job?" The Police Sergeant nods his head, "Yes?" Felice cries, "Well Tommy and these guys didn't. They went out night after night and kept the streets safe for everyone. The loyal ones like Tommy never took a dime for doing it! They were like superheroes; nobody does that for anybody today! I can't believe it! You say to serve and protect?" she shakes her head, "and you were told to sweep it under the rug?" The Police Sergeant gets up and moves closer to Felice, "Hey, listen, Felice, it wasn't me. I wasn't assigned to that case at that time. There were a lot of crooked cops in here at that time, including that chief of Police! It's a lot different now! If I were in charge now, that bastard Sassy would have been off the streets the first time he touched anyone, believe me! Please Felice, I know this is very hard for you, but I must know more about the relationship you've had with Tommy. What he was like? How he was to you?" The Sargent moves back to his desk and checks through his paperwork as Felice begins to tell her story again. "It was odd timing, or fate or something, that's how it felt to me because Tommy had been with E-6 for a few years at that time, and things were changing with them, and at the same time, Tommy and I had so much love for one another even though we were together a short time at that time we both knew we were meant to be together for life anyway that's what I had felt inside for him, We were ready to go to the next level in the relationship."

SEVENTEEN

True Love

Tommy and Felice sit in the living room on the floor of Ashlie's apartment; they talk. Tommy takes a swig of his small bottle of whiskey he has in his hand. He leans up against the sofa as Felice sits beside him. The news is on in the background, the newscaster talks about the recent gang activity around Chicago and briefly mentions E-6 Thunder's vigilantism. Tommy looks at the T.V., waiting for Felice to say something about it, but she doesn't say a word about it. Tommy changes the subject, taking a swig of whiskey, "So what about college boy?" Felice looks at him, "Nothing really, except he'll be here over the weekend."

Tommy looks at her, "You don't love him, do you?" Felice looks down and slowly raises her head and slowly shakes it, "No..." She looks at Tommy, "How did you know?" Tommy leans forward towards her, "I just know things like that." The sexual tension builds between them, and Felice's heart begins to race. Tommy pulls her towards him, and he kisses her. Felice has a hard time but stops softly, "No, please, Tommy, not yet... Let me tell Richie first." Felice's heart beats so fast, out of breath. "I think it's the right thing to do. I will tell him tomorrow." Tommy knows Felice is a one-of-a-kind young woman, backs off and leans back in a sitting position and doesn't say a word, nods his head, "ok" Felice gets up, stopping herself but sexually charged, "I think I'm gonna go to sleep." She walks out of the room. Tommy was looking at the T.V., "Good night!" Felice feels quite foolish, but having traditional values on the bed doesn't say anything.

The following day, Tommy sleeps on the couch at Five Thirty A.M. Felice is in her bedroom also sleeping, and Ashlie is in her bedroom under the sheets, having sex with her boyfriend. The sound of the bed banging up

against the wall wakes Felice up. She gets up to open Ashlie's door and sees them. Felice shakes her head and smiles and quickly closes the door before they can see her. Then she goes to check on Tommy, who is still asleep. She walks into the kitchen to make Tommy lunch for work. Ashlie now walks out of her bedroom. Her boyfriend, whose name is "Joe," follows her and stands at her side, Ashlie, standing there looking very sexy, says, "Felice you know my boss from work, don't you?" "Joe, this is Felice. Felice my boss Joe!" Felice turns and almost laughs in his face, and Ashlie points Joe to the bathroom, "There's the bathroom!" Joe to Felice, "Nice to see you again!" shuts the door to the bathroom, both girls LAUGH. Felice whispering, "Your boss!!?? What about?" referring to Ashlie's ex-boyfriend, Ashlie replies, "He's old news, 'NO GOOD IN THE SACK!'" Felice shakes her head and laughs quietly, "Yeah, but...?" Ashlie Whispers, "Yeah, Joe has been hitting on me for a while, and yesterday at lunchtime everybody left he asked me to stay, and we banged our brains out in his office, and that ain't even the worst part. He's married, and he has two kids, but I told him I'm not looking for a relationship right now, so he can have me, in the day and go back to play house at night with his wife, He told his wife last night he had to stay at work overnight to do something important.... which was me! But she doesn't know that! Felice, he is so great in bed too! Talk about having fringe benefits!" They both burst out laughing. Felice continues to shake her head, "I don't know about you Ash..." Ashlie begins to walk into her room and sees Tommy sleeping on the sofa, "And Felice, you better watch Tommy, he's one fine piece! When I'm through with Joe, he's next on my list!" Felice pointing her finger at Ashlie, whispering, "You better play nice, he's mine! Keep away from him." Ashlie whispers back to her, "Ok, I'm only playing. I know how you feel for him, I will be good!" again they laugh, Felice gets serious, "Hey listen Ash do you think it would be ok if Tommy stays here for a few days, he's been practically sleeping on the street he will give you some money!" Ashlie nods her head, "Sure! No problem." Felice continues to make lunch for Tommy, Ashlie gets dressed for work, and Joe is still in the shower, a few minutes pass by. Joe and Ashlie come out of the bedroom together, Felice tops both of them. "Would you like me to make you both something

before you go to work?" Ashlie being funny, "No, we're both late looks at Joe, we may get fired!" They all laugh. Joe looks at his watch, "Let's go though we are really late!" Ashlie smiles, "ok, Fe, I'll see you later." The two walk out the door, Joe to Felice, "Bye good seeing you again!" Felice nods her head to him, and she shuts the door and laughs, "Oh my god Ash!"

A few minutes pass, Felice Is getting ready to go to work. She takes a shower. The shower stops and Felice begins to dry herself off. She opens the bathroom door fast and Tommy is standing there. Felice is startled for a moment. She is in nothing but a towel. Felice smiles, and covers herself up quickly, "Oh, hi sleepyhead." Tommy looked very tired, grins, "What's up sexy? Could I use the shithouse for a while?" Felice smiles, "Sure, if you put it that way! But open the window and use the spray!" They both stare at one another for a moment. Felice's cell phone rings. Their eyes locked on one another. Felice walks past Tommy, "I need to get that. It'll be a minute."

As Felice gets her phone, Tommy goes into the bathroom to wash his face but stops to listen to Felice's phone conversation. Tommy leans up against the sink. Felice grabs her phone, that is on her bed. Felice answers it, "Hello? Oh, Richie hi. Yeah, I know I said I would call you, but I had something really important to do. Can we see each other tonight?" she pauses for a moment while he speaks, "No, not that! It's about us. What time can I see you?" Another short pause, "Well, I get out at five. Ok, I'll be outside the campus gates around six. Bye!"

Felice seems very unsure of how to handle the situation. Tommy, from the bathroom, heard the whole conversation, just standing quietly in the bathroom. Felice walks in the kitchen, leans up against the counter, with her head down, "Tommy?" Felice walks over to the bathroom and opens the door. She sees Tommy standing there without a shirt. "Oh, I'm sorry!" Tommy with a towel in his hands, "No, that's ok. What is it?" Felice, unsure of herself, "Well Richie just called, and I just told him I'd be there at six o'clock tonight, but I really don't know what to say to him. He's a total

ass and I don't want to be with him anymore!" Tommy with a rebellious manner, "give it to him straight!" Felice hesitantly, "Can you maybe come with me tonight?" Felice walks over to him, "Please?" Tommy nods his head, "Yeah, I don't care." Felice hugs him, "Oh, Tommy, thanks!" Again, Tommy gives Felice a long passionate kiss. But this time Felice doesn't pull away. Tommy just looks at her, "I have to get out of here." Walks away from her, looking back, "I'll see you tonight!" He walks out the door. Felice looks up, "Oh my God!"

EIGHTEEN

Felice's decision

That night at five forty-five p.m.,

Tommy pulls up in front of the diner where Felice works, using Big Vic's brand new black on black Lincoln continental, he waits outside for a few minutes, talking on his cell phone to an unknown caller, probably someone in the ranks of E-6 thunder, Felice nervous but excited about what she is going to do, that is break it off with Richie, And spend the rest of her life with her one true love Tommy, she walks out of the diner and looks in the car at Tommy on the phone talking she smiles, Tommy is dressed to the tee, she looks at him. Tommy on the phone, "I'm going over there now to see him, OK? bye!" Tommy hangs up his phone, Felice looks at Tommy, "what a car?" Tommy replies, "It's Big Vic's!" Felice, "Does he mind you using it?" Tommy smiles, "As long as I don't total it, I'm fine!" Tommy drives faster, Felice holds on, "Oh God I Shouldn't have said anything!" Tommy laughs as he drives, Tommy looks in the rear-view mirror, "I just have to make a quick stop first!" Felice smiles, "I don't care make Richie wait! he deserves it!" Tommy nods his head, "Aah, now you're talking!" Tommy now pulls down a street of tenement apartments, a guy awaits at the door, standing on the front steps, Tommy to Felice, "I'll be right back, keep the doors shut and locked, Fe!" Felice nods her head, "Okay!" Tommy walks up to the guy and begins to talk to him, the guy is very disheveled looking, Felice puts the window down a bit so she can hear what he is talking about... Tommy pulling the guy close to him, the guy has four screaming children around him which are his, Tommy looks at him, "Hey stan, you can't keep doing this, man, you got to get off that shit and get into rehab, and stop fuckin gambling, I cover for you because you have kids and all, but Big Vic and Gatch, said this is the last time!"

Stan cries, "I know! I gotta, Tommy, but it's easier said than done." Tommy replies, "It's not me, Big Vic say's you're making a mockery out of him!" Stan yells to his wife, "Put these kids in the house damnit!" Stan's wife comes out and takes the kids in the house, she looks at Tommy. Now Tommy reaches into his pocket and takes out a wad of money, Tommy shakes his head, "Look at the way you got your family living. Come on! No more!" hands him the money, "This is the last time!" Felice still listens from the car, Tommy walking back to the car... Felice quickly puts the window back up, Tommy shouts to Stan, "Get your shit together Bro! For your family's sake!" Tommy shakes his head as he gets into the car. Felice doesn't say a word, Tommy pissed to himself, "Some people I'm tellin' you?" He drives off.

As Tommy and Felice drive in the car, on their way to Richie's college, Felice looks nervous, Tommy holds her hand and looks at her, Felice a bit worried, "I hope everything goes, o.k.?" Tommy, looking ahead, "just be straight with him, like I said." They drive up to the campus gates and stop. Tommy looks at her, "Are you gonna be, ok?" Felice nervously nods her head, "Yeah... I have to stop being a little bitch and get this over with!" Tommy nods his head, "I'll tell you what, I'll be back in a half an hour, stay and talk to him, near the tables over there and I'll meet you on the steps on the other side and point his finger there, ok?" Felice hugs him, "thanks I would like that." Now Felice looks near the tables and see's Richie looking at them, Felice gets out of the car and shuts the door walking towards Richie, Tommy gives Richie a tough guy stare, Richie looking very intimidated, looks the other way, Tommy speeds off in the car.

Forty-five minutes later... Dusk, Felice and Richie are still talking at the tables and the lights are on outside, and just as he promised, Tommy sits on the steps supporting Felice and making his presence known to Richie not to fuck with Felice and let her go or pay the consequences. Felice is much more confident in herself than before, "Well, you and I know we are not going very far with this relationship, Richie. You honestly have no respect for me or anything that I do, you screw everything in sight,

and you treat me like shit!" Richie, not taking it very well, "I told you, I'm sorry that I cheated on you, besides it was only once." Felice getting mad, "Bullshit! All those numbers in your phone, the text messages, I've seen everything." Richie turns away, "What happened to you? You were never like this before?" Felice smiles, "I grew up, thank you for showing me that I had to push myself not to be treated like an asshole by you or anyone, besides see all your thinking right now is yourself and nobody else but you! I was never in your equation, you just wanted a trophy, I'm sorry I'm not going to be that!" Richie looks over at Tommy. And Tommy continues to stare at him. Richie with one more last-ditch effort to convince "Felice, Ok, Ok, maybe I do treat you like shit, but you'll want me back one day and you know it!" shakes his head, "When I'm filthy frigging rich!" Felice shakes her he'd, "I don't think so! No, I know so! I never loved you anyway, Richie! I can't believe how immature a college person could be!" Felice turns and starts to walk away. Richie grabs her arm, looks as though he's about to cry, "Please don't leave me Felice, stay with me tonight, like you used to!" Felice breaks free and begins to walk away back to Tommy, "Stop groveling Richie you sound pathetic." As she gets further away. Richie cries and shouts to her, "But I love I Felice..., F E L I C E!" He shouts.

NINETEEN

The Passion

In the car ride home, Felice is very quiet, not because she is upset, but rather relieved that she can take her relationship with Tommy to the next level, without feeling the guilt she has had prior. Tommy, concerned about her, holds her hand, and looks at her. "Are you alright Fe?" Tommy reaches in the back of the car and takes out a dozen of red and white long-stemmed roses. Felice, shocked, nods her head, feeling good about this transition, "Yeah! How could anything be wrong?" She looks at Tommy as the moon shimmers behind her in the nighttime sky.

Back at the apartment, Felice's room, the lighting is very dim, Tommy and Felice stand close to one another, staring into each other's eyes. Tommy runs his hand through her long, beautiful hair, Felice looking straight into Tommy's eyes. "Tommy, I always loved you. Even when we were kids, I knew that one day we would be together. Like you said, it was meant to be. I'll always love you!" Tommy grabs her and kisses her passionately. They make love. Later... Tommy and Felice are in each other's arms... She looks at him and says, "Tommy please don't ever hurt me!" Tommy, very sincere, looks at her and replies, "You're my best friend, I would die for you Fe, you know that!" The next morning, Felice is asleep, Tommy gets up to get ready for work, he walks over to Felice and covers her with a blanket and puts yet another rose on her nightstand next to her.

Back to the present day...

Felice looks down, with a slight smile on her face, "We made love everywhere, and every time we could it was always great, he was so passionate." Frank shakes his head and turns away for a moment, finding

it hard to take in..... Felice continues, laughs, stares out the window, "I also dragged him to art shows all over the place, but he loved it though! We snuck into almost everywhere for free, and other times all he had to tell them who he was with or flash his colors and we'd get right in, it was unbelievable!"

Back to the past...,

Tommy and Felice walk through an art gallery, Tommy walking, looking down at the ground, while Felice looks at artwork, "So how did you get interested in art Fe?" "Well when I was really young, my father was an art teacher for a while in high school. I don't know if you remember that. But anyway, he used to take me with him on the weekends and teach people, and it just stuck with me, laughing but I always had more paint on my hands and face then I did on the paper or canvas!" Tommy smiles and raises his hands, "Hey look mom Aaah!" Felice laughs, Tommy Gets serious, "No, but you should do something with it, your work kicks the crap they have on the walls here..." Felice nods her head, "Yeah, I wish I could but that's what I'm going to school for but it's taking such a long time, sometimes it gets so frustrating Ya, know? I'm more of a hands-on person, I guess I'm stuck at the diner and school for a while!" Tommy stops and looks at her, "Hey how about we room together? You could work less hours, and I can get a second job somewhere, so you can focus on your career, not your job!" Felice, "I couldn't do that to you Tommy, I mean I'd love to be with you and all, but...." Tommy in control, "Say no more babe It's done! I want to do this. You have amazing potential, hey look it's not going to get weird or anything, even though we're together now and all, there's still no strings attached, if you do get weirded out at any time, I will leave I promise." Felice looks into his eyes she nods her head and he grabs her close to him and they kiss.

Back to the present....

Felice with tears streaming down her face, "And that was it, that was how we started our own life together in our own apartment!"

TWENTY

Starting their own life together

Present day...

"So it actually took Me and Tommy a few weeks to get enough money for me to get out of Ashlie's apartment, she really didn't want me to go, she was a great friend laughs, I used to joke with her and say you don't care about me leaving you're just worried about the money you won't have extra when I'm gone right?" She said, "are you crazy?" "No, but we just got another one of our friends Samantha to split the rent with her, but after she moved in every time Ash and I hung out together, she always told me there was nothing like our friendship, we were like sisters! But when I moved in with Tommy, it was the best thing I ever did." "You know when some people hate who they're with? Tommy and I grew, I couldn't get enough of seeing him, although he was very complicated at times and our life wasn't perfect. I can just say we were just the perfect fit for one another. Everyone used to say it, even the guys from E-6 Thunder! They used to joke with Tommy and say he was whipped! But Tommy could take a joke and used to go back at them and say I've found the love of my life... You guys should be so lucky! But it was all good fun! Then when Ashlie settled down with one guy finally, Tommy took us to the clubs no waiting on lines, Even though Tommy wasn't a college boy, he fit right in with my crowd, But I used to get pissed off at Ashlie because no madder what She would flirt with Tommy, and make comments about him, Tommy assured me he wouldn't even give her the time of day, and just the way he looked at me, I totally believed him, and I told Ash how I felt about that and she stopped, but then I realized that's what I have to go through if I wanted to be with him, he was that infectious on everyone who met him, but in my head I knew he was mine and nobody else's! She smiles, "Remember,

I told you that Tommy told me he would get two jobs. Well, he did. He drove trucks, plus had his job at the furniture store, that guy worked so hard! Because he wanted me to finish my schooling, then he'd joke and say when you graduate you can take care of me women!" But I couldn't do that to him, so while he was at work, I made sure I was helping out working and making sure I had enough hours in the diner, and taking my school work there to study on downtime, and eventually everything began to fall into place with us financially that is, but his anger towards Steve slowly came out at times, and Tommy's darker sides came out..."

Tommy's demons

Present Day... Felice to sergeant, "I started to see, Tommy could be warm one minute and totally in his own world the next. Especially after we moved in together. Sometimes he could get very scary!"

Back in the past, Tommy and Felice are in their apartment in the living room on the floor. Tommy lies on his stomach reading Felice a book. Felice sits up, very interested in what Tommy is reading. Tommy slurs his words a bit as he reads, "So Bill's father always misunderstood him. He tried very hard all the time, but lack of communication made it almost impossible to do so." Tommy immediately stops reading, puts the book down, and rolls over onto his back. Felice knows something is wrong. "Why did you stop reading Tom? What's wrong?" Tommy very solemnly looks up at the ceiling, "That's the frigging way I feel about Steve Fe! Did you hear when kid Bill said his father was always putting him down, never giving him any confidence, he had to get it all himself." Tommy begins to brood a bit and gets up and goes into the bedroom. Felice gets up and goes after him. Felice is worried and stands next to him, "Tommy, are you o.k.?" Tommy was quite embarrassed, not waiting to show his emotions to Felice, "Yeah, I'll get over it! Let's get outta here! II want to take you somewhere!"

The present... Felice to sergeant, "And that's the way Tommy was, brooding one minute and sporadic the next? Very unpredictable! That night, Tommy stole a motorcycle, and we drove all around the city, but sometimes Tommy wouldn't speak to me for days at a time." Sergeant writing everything down, "and you lived with someone like that?" Felice looking down, "Well at first, I didn't know how to handle it. But as time went on, I started to see that he was trying to establish some kind of personality. I wasn't always with him when he was with E-6, but when we were alone, I felt his every emotion because it was easy for him to open up to me! It made me feel good because I knew he needed me and loved me! I would have gone through Hell and back for him and he knew it! Every night at school I spent hours on the computer looking up his parents for him to try to give him some closure in his life!"

TWENTY-ONE

Tommy's Demons Part Two

Twelve Noon, a very rainy and dreary day,

Tommy is driving the furniture delivery truck back to the warehouse, he is alone at the time, his cell phone rings, it's his boss on the other end, Tommy looks at the number, "Fuck, this is all I need now." Tommy answers his phone, "Hello?" The Boss was very stern, "Hey Cade, back to my office." Tommy not going to take any shit, "On my way, I'm around the corner!" (But takes some shit from his Boss for Felice's sake) Tommy pulls the huge truck into the yard, as rain pours down, his Boss stands outside waiting for him, Tommy parks the truck and he gets out and goes over to his Boss. The Boss has his clipboard in his hand, "Come inside for a sec, huh!" They walk into the warehouse, Tommy not liking this kind of authority at all, "Yeah what?" The Boss, showing his dislike for Tommy, "You need to do me a favor." Tommy, a tough guy, has his E-6 colors on, "What is it?" Boss replies, "You need to work for Ryan tomorrow night... straight through. Nobody wants to do it, so I guess you're elected. We're short today too, so I need you to stay till midnight." Tommy wants to blast him but thinking about Felice, "No prob! I GOT IT!" The Boss gets a little angry because he wants to get to Tommy. But Tommy plays it cool and just walks away without saying a word about it. The Boss infuriated, "Oh, Cade..." Tommy turns around, "What?" The Boss again replies, "Don't wear your colors to work anymore. It's bad for my business." Tommy, in a rebellious tone, "You're the boss!" Tommy just walks out of the warehouse and back to his truck.

Later that same night... One Thirty a.m., The Apartment,

Felice sleeps in bed, as Tommy Lies next to her on his back wide awake, staring at the ceiling. Tommy also suffers from insomnia, starts to think back to when he was a young boy at the age of ten. In his memory, he drifts back as Steve and Renee sit in their kitchen with a Special Ed teacher discussing Tommy's behavior at school. Little Tommy sits there solemnly, Steve very angry, gets up and walks around, "What do you mean?" The Teacher knows that Steve is a hothead, watches what she says to him, quite frightened, "Well Mr. and Mrs. Cade Tommy has a very complicated learning disability. I promise you I did all I can, but he just isn't responding. He's the last in the class, He's so I behind. A group of teachers and myself got together..." Steve pissed off cuts in, "Yeah, and what took an early lunch?" Renee concerned and angry at Steve, "Shut up Steve!" To the Teacher, "I'm sorry!" And we suggest to you, to put him in a special school. Renee looks at the teacher, very depressed, "Do you think it will help him?" Steve walks over to Tommy, getting right in his face, not caring who's there, "Are you crazy Renee? Huh? I wouldn't spend a fuckin' dime on him." SHOUTS, "He's not even ours! He's not even worth the damn time! Put him someplace." Looking straight at Tommy, "are you a retarded or something?" Renee YELLS, "Steve, what the hell are you saying to him, stop and take a look at what you are saying! We'll figure out what his problems are. He's a little slower than other kids, that's all." Turns to the Teacher, "I will do anything I can to help him...., Anything!" Steve, with no emotion, YELLS, "Shut the fuck up Renee! You're just as bad as him." Turns back to Tommy, "Do you hear what your teacher is telling us? Or are you too dumb to understand that? All the other kids are smarter than you! And you sit there like some sort of dunce, God damn it!" Steve hits Tommy. Renee and the Teacher yell for him to stop, trying to pull him off, both of them SHOUT. Little Tommy just sits there silently. The Teacher is very frightened, threatening to take Tommy out of the house, Renee pleads with her, "No! Please don't, Steve will leave before I make you take this child away. I love him very much!" Steve, ignoring what everyone else is saying, slams a book in front of Tommy. "What are you gonna grow up to be, a dummy? A retard? You'll never amount to anything! I HATE YOU!" Tommy puts his head down. Renee screams and runs out of the room

crying, "They're going to take him away from me! They're going to take him away from me!" Tommy just looks at Steve. Tommy slowly comes back into the present time, with a sad look on his face, rolls over, Felice still asleep, he hits his fist on the floor and drifts off and goes to sleep.

TWENTY-TWO

What E-6 is made of

Felice in the Police station...Tommy began to tell me of all of his horrible nightmares, his demons, that he felt that haunted him, that's when he told me that's why E-6 Thunder meant so much to him about what they stand for. The less fortunate, the nobodies, the misunderstood, He would do anything for E-6! They were one of a kind! Most men... Most People wish they could have had the heart... and... BALLS these guys had for other human beings! Like I said, although it wasn't right, the way they handled things, I guess it gave Tommy a sense of closure for him, that he was helping the helpless! slowly fade into the past, I remember one night we were out, at dinner with Ashlie and her boyfriend we were laughing, drinking, and talking about something we've seen on T.V., And Tommy's phone rings, he checked the number and he had the look of concern on his face... He gets up and whispers in my ear that Big Vic needed to see him right away, Tommy to Ashlie and her boyfriend, I'm sorry I have to go! Turns to Felice, I'm sorry Fe, I need to go see somebody! Felice, somewhat disappointed, nods her head, and mouths the words to him 'I LOVE YOU!' Tommy nods his head and walks away.

Felice for the moment back to the present...

It really scared me because every time he left like that, I felt that "Will I ever see him again!"

Tommy drives to the club where a lot of E-6 Thunder members are including Big Vic, Tommy walks through the crowds of People who are dancing, to get to Big Vic who is standing at the bar with a couple of women, Big Vic turns around, Big Vic smiles, hugs him, "Hey Tommy!

how are you, come on, I have something to discuss with you in the back room?" Tommy nods his head, "Okay!" The women that were talking to Big Vic, stare at Tommy and say how good looking he is, Big Vic and Tommy walk to the back rooms, passing people having sex, and partying. The two guys walk into a vacant room with just a table and two chairs in it, Big Vic says, "sit down Tommy, I have something to discuss with you." Tommy grabs a chair, In Big Vic sits in the other. Very seriously, "I have another huge problem..., Big! And you know you're the only motherfucker I trust! It's one of our own!" Gets mad, "You know Chickie, right?" Tommy nods his head, "Yeah, I crossed paths with him a couple of times." Big Vic, "Yeah, get this, he was dating an underage girl, the parents didn't approve, but this cocksucker, got a big head and pushing his E-6 muscle around, and ignored them, the girl took so much shit from her parents that she decided to listen to them, and broke it off with that fuckin' piece of shit, Chickie takes a gun and barges into the house, shoots the parents not killing them though and takes the girl upstairs to her room and rapes her... And I found out that he shouted E-6made me do this! I want that FUCKER DEAD! Make him pay for it, no mercy! But don't do it tonight! I want you to stalk him a bit, follow him for the next couple of days, I want you Stats, Nuch, and Sal Blondie, to do this one. Yeah, he won't suspect Sal Blondie, because he was pretty close with him, I can't believe I let that motherfucker in E-6, he's smearing our good name!" Tommy is very calm, "don't worry Vic, it will be done." Big Vic nods his head, "I know it will be Tommy. Thanks, I owe you! Hey if we couldn't rely on ourselves, who can we rely on? Right?" Laughs, "God knows we can't rely on the crooked cops out there." "Anyway the soon to be dead Chickie, is in the club tonight somewhere do me a favor and go see if you can find him and watch him..., Then tell the guys what's about to go down in the next few days." Tommy nods his head, "Got It!"

Tommy walks out of the room and goes into the club on the dance floor... And walks around a bit, walking through the people who are dancing. He walks around near the bar where He spots Chickie talking and dancing with a few women trying to get with them. Chickie laughs like he doesn't

have a care in the world, Tommy notices that he has a short-sleeve shirt on with a whole tattoo sleeve dedicated to the E-6 thunder, ink on it. Tommy stares intently at it, but making sure Chickie doesn't suspect anything. Then Tommy walks around the club finding Nuch, Sal Blondie, and Stats, standing in the foreground as Tommy goes over what they are going to do to Chickie, in the next couple of days…, as they all intently watch Chickie as he parties it up with the women.

Two days later…, Chickie's Apartment, ONE FORTY-FIVE a.m., Without warning Tommy bangs on the door, Standing in back of him are the guys, and because Sal Blondie is a good friend of Chickie, Tommy signals to him to call his name, Sal Blondie with no emotion, "Hey Chickie open up, It's Sal!" Chickie replies, "ONE MINUTE!" Half crocked Chickie opens the door, "Hey Blondie what's up?" And the four of them push their way into the apartment door, Tommy has a cord in his hand and wraps it around Chickie's neck and drags him to the chair. Out of the bedroom come two women, very scared, they run out of the apartment, Nuch shouts to them, "GET OUTTA HERE BITCHES! DON'T YOU KNOW THIS MOTHERFUCKER RAPED AN UNDERAGE GIRL AND HE'S GONNA PAY NOW!" Chickie begins to cry, "What do you mean, man?" Tommy very serious, "Don't play fuckin dumb you know what you did!" Stats jumps in, "You know what you did fuck job, there's no room for you in E-6…" Chickie knows what's coming, "Sal… Blondie?" Sal Blondie just looks at him in disgust and shakes his head, "nobody's gonna save you now!" Chickie looks at Tommy as he sits and just stares at Chickie, Tommy almost sinisterly like, "You put your own needs before protecting others? You know that's not what E-6 is about. Do you know what you did to that girl and her family? How could you betray the whole E-6 family? Did you really think you were going to get away with this? You know, Big Vic and Gatch are going to expand around the country and murder fuckin' scum like you, I might take a picture and send it on the internet on the torture we're going to do to you, I bet the innocent will be fuckin glad to see a fucker like yourself murdered by the good guys, scumbags like you will think twice before you harm somebody!" "You shot the girl's parents in the face, point blank,

and took the girl upstairs and fuckin raped her, and put them in critical condition. All three of them? That family is a mess now. And what do you think Big Vic and Gatch think about as your raping the girl, you shout out E-6 made me do it? What the hell was that? And if they do come out of this, you don't think they're not going to press charges against you, then 5-0 comes down on E-6 when they have a bad day at the office? Thinking we're the bad guys! Or maybe you thought we were going to harbor you?" Chickie goes to his knees like the scum that he is and pleads for his life, Tommy begins to smack him around, Tommy holding him down, strip him of his colors! And burn the clothes right here! Nuch and Stats begin to strip Chickie as he pleads, "Please, please, I loved her!" Tommy angered, "You know you're a sick motherfucker!" Stats takes the colors and throws them in the corner of the room and Sal Blondie, take the lighter fluid out from his jacket and lights them on fire! Tommy begins to choke the life out of Chickie, Sal Blondie runs from the corner to the bed and shouts to Chickie, "YOU GOTTA GO BRO! You're better off us killing you now, who wants to rot in a jail cell all alone anyway right?" screaming in his ear. Tommy lets go of the severely bloodied Chickie for a moment as all four of them begin to beat him to a pulp, Tommy bends down to Chickie and they stop for a moment, Tommy grabs Chickie by the hair, "We're getting you all pretty for you to get to Hell..., DO YOU KNOW WHAT THEY CALL ME?" Chickie out of breath replies, "I heard they call you the Angel of Death!" Tommy nods his head..., "That's right Mother fucker!" Chickie out of air, bloodied and near death, Tommy takes out a butcher's knife and grabs Chickie's arm with the E-6 Ink on it, Chickie screams for his life as Tommy begins to carve the tattoo out taking chunks of his skin with it, Tommy shouts at Chickie, "You know you're a disgrace to E-6 thunder!" Chickie screams in sheer agony as the rest of the guy's watch, Chickie with one last breath, "Can't you be the Angel of mercy? and let me go? PLEASE!!" He cries and shouts, Tommy calmly looks at him and replies, "Were you that girl's Angel of Mercy when you raped and made her beg for her life? NO!" Stats takes out a gun and shoots Chickie right in the head. Blood spies everywhere..., meanwhile the fire in the room builds the four guys grab blankets and smother the fire until it is out..., Tommy

Shouts, "THROW THIS PIECE OF SHIT OUT THE WINDOW!" Sal Blondie opens the window and the four of them toss the lifeless body out the window and it hits the sidewalk, passers-by scream in horror. Tommy and E-6 exit through a fire door.

Felice Present day..., That made crazy headlines...

Police sergeant, "I know I remember that one clear as day." Thinks "My daughter was born the next day..., and all I could think about was what if that happened to her one day?" What would I have done if that was someone from my own family..., Felice nods her head looking at the Officer, "You would have done the same thing right? Now you're getting it!" Tears in her eyes, "they weren't the bad guys!"

Felice continues..., And the most publicized and biggest incidents with E-6 was with a mother who reached out to E-6 because of a sixteen-year-old boy who was gay and was so depressed he began to cut himself numerous times. He was tormented a bullied in school, and came home to be equally tormented and then beaten by his own father, this kid had no one to turn to except his mother he was about to end his life, and the mother was so on the brink she had no job or money beaten and raped by her husband. Many E-6 members took money from their own pockets, set the mother and son up in their own apartment, got her a job, made an example of the father who is now in prison for beating his son for gay bashing him... And today this kid is now in college and is set to go to law school and is in a great relationship all because somebody cared for them! I would know because I counsel them both today! Isn't that what this life is supposed to be about? Helping the next person, this is what should make headlines for people to take notice of this world! This is why E-6 Thunder are legends today!

Then it hit close to home..., As Tommy was working double shifts, I began to work later and later at the Twenty-four hour diner..., like I said before there was this out-of-town business guy that kept coming around every

time he was in Chicago, he was creepy, at first I thought he was harmless until he started really hitting on me, I didn't tell Tommy because I knew what he would do to him if he got his hands on him, so I let it go for a while, I figured I could handle myself pretty good, but then hitting on me turned to touching me...,

Felice drifts into the past...

TWENTY-THREE

Hitting Home

Three Thirty a.m.

The diner has hardly anyone in it, and the few that are in there were either coming back from partying, or truckers on the road looking for food after a long haul. The businessman who was flirting with Felice walks into the diner again and is very persistent in getting her, this is the fourth time in a week that he has been in. He's in his late thirties, well-groomed, good looking and very cocky, sits in a booth and constantly stares at Felice's every move making him very creepy, the businessman points his finger at her, "Hey Felice come here!" Felice walks over to him, "How do you know my name? I didn't give it out!" The businessman looks at her, "whoa, don't get so mad babe, I just asked around, that's all!" Felice getting angry, "please don't call me babe, I'm not your babe!" The businessman smiles, "hey look, I've been coming in here for over a month now, just for you, my name is Elliot and I'm from California, and I'm here on business, for a big corporate deal, I have a shitload of money, I'm married with two kids back at home..., but all I keep thinking about is you, and what I would like to do with you..."

Felice begins to get freaked out, "Hey listen, you need to get out of here!" Elliot puts his hand over her, "But why? There's no harm in just talking.... About sex! Wait Felice, you have one of the greatest asses I've ever seen! I'm so fuckin horny right now, I wish I could put you up on that counter right here!" The cook at the diner notices that Felice is having trouble and walks over to the table. The Cook has a bat in his hand, "What's the problem over here Felice, go in the back. I'll take care of him." Felice has tears in her eyes, embarrassed, walks away to the back of the diner, the

Cook to Elliot waving the bat, "You have a fuckin problem? Get the fuck out of here and leave my waitresses alone, you crackpot, I'll fuckin bust your scull open and serve it for lunch tomorrow!" Elliot, not taking threats very well, reluctantly gets up, and begins to walk out of the diner not before shouting out to Felice, "SEE YOU AROUND FELICE!" He smiles and walks out the door, the Cook turns around, "people are fuckin animals today!" The few people that are in the diner look on and say good job to the cook, Felice walks out from behind the counter and walks over to him and says, "Thank you!" The Cook replied with a smile, "It's your fault you know! Why did you have to be so frigging beautiful?!" Felice laughs, shakes her head, and walks away.

That same night, four forty-five a.m......,

Felice now is at the end of her shift, she counts her tips, Felice says to the cook, "Manny I'm on my way out!" Manny says to her, "Okay Felice do you want me to walk you out." Felice preoccupied at the moment still counting her money, "No I'm Okay, Tommy should be here in a minute!" Manny replies, "See you tomorrow!" Felice walks out the door, and she looks around as it is almost sunrise, Tommy texts her on her phone and says he'll be there in a few, the street is an eerie calm. Up from behind her comes Elliot, who says, "Don't say a fuckin' word, Felice!" Felice, who doesn't know what hit her, tries to break free but Elliot is too strong for her and forces her into a nearby alley. As he puts her hand up her skirt and tries to rip her panties off, Elliot, angry, "See what you're making me do? Felice, I'm not a rapist! I'm just so fuckin' horny for you! Please let me put it in you! I can give you everything you would want! Money, diamonds." Felice screams, "NO!" Elliot throws her to the ground, and jumps on top of her..., Like a lunatic Elliot almost in his own world presses himself up against Felice and says, "Do you feel how hard I am for you right now?" Felice screams, "get off me!" She fights as much as she can and punches him square in the jaw. Now in back of them car lights are seen, and a car makes a screeching noise, and Tommy jumps out of the car, and without saying a word grabs onto Elliot's shirt and pulls him off and begins to

beat on him, Tommy threw him up against the brick wall of the diner, Felice knowing Tommy will kill him screams and tries to pull him off, but Tommy doesn't respond and continues to beat on him, and he pulls a gun out of his pocket Tommy to Elliot, "OPEN YOUR FUCKIN' MOUTH!" "Tommy no! Don't kill him! You'll go to jail!" The few people that are in the diner, including Manny, come running out of the diner, Manny runs over to Tommy and grabs his shoulders and say's "It's over Tommy..., Let him go! You don't need this!" Felice cries, "Tommy! Tommy!" drops Elliot to the ground, Elliot is so badly beaten, he can hardly move. Tommy looks at him and spits on him, "You piece of shit! Nobody touches my girl! Ever!" He puts the gun away in his jacket, now the police cars roll up and 5-0 get out of their cars. Tommy shouts, "SHOWS OVER GET THE HELL OUT OF HERE!"

Felice present day...,

Tommy saved my life that night! Who knows what would have happened? We spent the night at the Police station, pointing her finger, "Right over there! I can still see my knight sitting there, not giving the crooked cops anything, miraculously they let us go, but they told us don't leave town, I think Big Vic paid off some of the cops to turn the other way, It worked but the 5-0 told us Tommy was going to have a hearing in the upcoming days and if he was found guilty he would have to serve some time. Could you believe that I was almost raped, and he saves me, and he might have had to do time? It doesn't make sense. 'Justice?'"

A few weeks went by, and we were both waiting to hear something. I went back to work at the diner, and it was quiet. "Thank God!" Tommy did the craziest thing. He came into the diner and handed me two pieces of paper, on them one said, "You" and the other said "Choose!" and told me that he loves me and walked out of the diner; stunned as usual by him, I opened the one note which contained a job offer for a graphic artist, and the other was for a counselor to help people in need. Tommy said, "it was a gift from him because I was graduating college in the next few weeks,

I was totally stunned by it." We were everything together, and I'm nothing without him. I graduated with honors, and I chose to counsel over art, because I feel the need to help troubled people, Kids, Teens, and Adults, I put off art until a later date, It was a funny thing because I felt if I took Art it would be selfish of me, and I didn't want to be that person I'm glad I made that choice to become what I've become, and you know I wouldn't have it any other way, Felice stops and looks at her mother and father. Somewhat making them feel foolish on the way they have acted through the years.

TWENTY-FOUR

A Brighter Outlook Turns Grim

Months pass and nothing surfaced yet about the brutal beating Tommy had given the businessman Elliot, which is a good thing but is also hurting Tommy's job because he has to stay local and can't drive the truck, so he is confined to the warehouse, something Tommy doesn't enjoy because his boss constantly giving him shit and is around all the time doing so... On the other hand, Felice's job of counseling is working out great, working with inner-city families helping and placing them in housing, and finding jobs for them. She feels she owes Tommy her life and would go through anything with or for him.

Tommy's job in the warehouse, Tommy is with another guy loading a huge breakfront on one of the trucks, as he is doing this he notices his boss on the floor with his partners in his business laughing, and occasionally shouting at his workers, Tommy see's this and gets somewhat angered at his boss and the way he is treating his employee's, Tommy drops what he is doing and walks over to the boss, "I need to talk to you!" The Boss shouting to some of his workers, "Come on! Move it! Time is money, people!" Then look at Tommy, "What do you want Cade?" Tommy was very frustrated, "I need to talk to you in your office." The Boss nods his head, "Okay..., let's go!" To the employees, "If I see anyone slacking, they're out the door." To his partner, "watch them!" The partner, "Got it!" The Boss and Tommy walk to his office, the boss closes the door and sits in his chair as Tommy stands in front of the desk. The Boss, very rude, "So what do you want?" Tommy stands there with his hands in his pockets, "Well for starters you should treat your employees a little bit better, they run this place for you, and two I'm your best worker, you're not finding anyone like me.... I need a raise!" The Boss was mad, "You know, I hate it when punks

like you come in here and think when you say that! You're a dime a dozen. Usually I'd fire someone like you but it just so happens I'm short of help and I know you know this and because of my bad fuckin luck I can't lose you right now, so I guess you win! A buck more than an hour." Tommy Smirks, "Two bucks more." The Boss, sits back in his chair, "Get to work!" Tommy, still smirking knowing he won the battle, turns around without saying anything and walks out of the office.

EIGHT THIRTY-FIVE p.m., That same night, the warehouse, Tommy is unloading a truck by himself, He turns to the huge drop off/loading door, and sees his Boss and two well-dressed men walk up talking to him at first Tommy ignores them. Then he notices them staring at him as he works, this goes on for a few minutes, until Tommy turns and sees a badge on one of the men and now knows they are Detectives. The first detective calls to Tommy, "Mr. Cade Tommy? May we have a word with you?" Tommy stops what he is doing and then turns towards them, and realizes this must be because of the businessman's situation, making them walk to him. "What's up?" Detective two shows Tommy his badge, I'm Detective Rhodes and this is Detective Goodman of the Chicago Police Department. Detective Two looks at Tommy, Yeah, that's the description. Detective One, "Can you please come with us, Tommy?" The detective takes out his cuffs. The Boss looks around, then to Tommy, "What the hell is going on here cade, huh?" Then he turns to the detectives, "Hey listen detective, I have my issues with cade, but he is one of my best workers!" Tommy doesn't say a word and just looks at his boss. Then the boss gets mad at him, "Hey Cade, I told you before I run a respectful business here!" The first detective reads Tommy his rights, as the other turns Tommy around with his back to him and cuffs him. Tommy puts up a bit of a struggle, "There's no need for this! I know what I did, Get this shit off me!" Detective One, "Come on Tommy, don't make this harder on yourself!" Workers begin to watch what is going on as they take Tommy away, The Boss yells as they put Tommy in the car, "NOW WHAT AM I GOING TO DO DETECTIVES?" Tommy looks at his Boss as they put him in the car. Now

the Boss Turns to his workers, "It's over! GET BACK TO WORK PEOPLE! CHARLIE COME OVER HERE AND TAKE CADE'S SPOT!"

One hour later...

The Police station. The two Detectives walk Tommy into the station. They sit him down on a bench. Tommy sits slumped on the bench with his head down. He is silent. The Detectives do paperwork on him, forty-five minutes go by, and Felice comes running through the door and goes right to Tommy's side, Felice, kneeling in front of him, "Tommy I talked to them, this is about that guy in the diner that night." Tommy looks at her, "I know, these bitches don't give you any info! I figured it out myself as soon as things are looking up, something always bites me in the ass! Hey, listen Fe, do me a favor, and get in touch with big Vic and tell him what's going on, I don't want them to come after me because they'll think I'm deserting them, I don't need that on me too!" Felice Looks at him with tears in her eyes, "Okay, I'll do that!" Now the Detective comes walking out of his office. Are you a friend of Tommy? Felice looks at the detective, "Yes, I'm Felice Levito!" The Detective looks at his sheet, "Oh Ms. Levito, you need to stay here for questioning also, please don't go anywhere. Give me a few minutes!" The detective walks away. Felice shaken up, "Tommy?" Tommy slumping on the bench, "they're really going to nail my ass to the ground this time, Fe!" He smiles with a helpless look on his face. Felice is very supportive of Tommy, "Don't worry Tommy, I'm with you for life, I'll get you out of this!"

Now another officer escorts the businessman in the doors of the police station, almost immediately see's and reacts to Tommy and Felice, SHOUTS, "That's them, He's the gangbanger that jumped me! And that's his bitch! I was minding my own business in that diner, and she came onto me; later that night outside that same diner, he attacked me from nowhere." Tommy without saying a word, got up still in handcuffs and lunged at the businessman "Elliot!" Felice screams, the two Detectives come running out of their offices and jump in to try and control Tommy's

rage, Felice Yells for Tommy, "No Tommy, that's what he wants you to do! Please don't! Stop!" Tommy kicks through everything in his way. It takes about six or seven officers to restrain him. Eventually, the officers do their job and bring Elliot to safety. Felice is crying and screaming. The Detective sits on Tommy, struggling with him. "Okay, tough guy, calm down!" A police sergeant walks out..., To the officers, "Throw him in cell four!" Felice cries, "No! Tommy!!!!" The Detectives pick up and take Tommy out. As Felice cries and follows them, Tommy struggles with the cops, "Fuck you! corrupt mother fuckers!" Tommy rants and raves like a madman, still trying to kick them, they succeed and reach the cell doors, opening them and throwing him in, Tommy falls to the floor and lays there silently. Officer one to other officer, "Is this guy on any narcotics?" officer two, shakes his head, "NO! He was tested clean earlier!" Officer one, shakes his head, "Man, I would hate to see what he'd be like on them, He's strong!" Officer two, laughs, "You're just getting old!" Felice pounds on the cell doors, "TOMMY!" Officer two grabs Felice under her arm, "Come on Ms. Levito, calm down. Let him think about what he did!" Felice cries hysterically for Tommy, "That's just it, Tommy didn't do anything but protect me!" The two officers take Felice away as they do so. She cries, "No, I can't leave him. I want to stay with him, He needs me! I need him! Please don't!"

TWENTY-FIVE

The Innocent Standalone

Two weeks pass... A civil court setting, Felice awaits in the courtroom with many other people awaiting their loved ones' fate.

A Court Bailiff shouts..., "NEXT CASE IS WERNER V.S. CADE!" Tommy is brought in handcuffs with an officer nearby him, and Tommy is sat down in the chair next to the judge's stand Felice sits on a chair and is very nervous. The prosecutor starts right in on Tommy. He turns to the judge, walking back and forth. "Your honor, this is an open and shut case! It's clear to see that you would have to judge this case in favor of my client who is a respected and successful businessman, who had come to our windy city innocently enough only to be beaten and viciously attacked and mugged by this man on the stand, Tommy Cade. He is a brutal gangbanger in an unknown set. He will not give up any information we know in this courtroom that what good are street gangs but trouble, right? And what street gangs don't have prior arrests against them and are all trouble! This individual, (points to him) Tommy Cade, who has a history of mental illness and violence in the past."

Felice jumps from her seat and SHOUTS, "THAT'S A DAMN LIE!" The judge shouts to Felice, "THAT'S STRIKE ONE FOR YOU MISS!" Go on, prosecutor.

Tommy slumped in the chair, slowly lifting his head and looking at Felice. They stare at each other. Felice is about to cry. The prosecutor nods his head, "Thank you, your honor. I'm sorry, your honor, I find it hard to talk to him because Mr. Cade is slumping in the seat!" The judge, "Permission granted, Mr. Cade, can you please sit up in your seat please and look at the prosecutor when he is talking to you!" Tommy very arrogantly doesn't

move. The judge hits his gavel, "MR. CADE, DID YOU HEAR ME? SIT UP AND LOOK AT THE PROSECUTOR WHEN TOLD TO DO SO!" Tommy continues to ignore the judge and his orders, his head down and still slumped in his seat, Felice sadly and softly to herself, "Please Tommy, don't do this to yourself listen to them!" The judge YELLS, "Bailiff, get sit him up, the right way now!" The Bailiff literally picks Tommy up and makes him sit the right way, then the bailiff returns to the corner of the room, The Prosecutor walks back up to Tommy, "Ok, Mr. Cade, state where you are from?" Tommy stammers, and smiles, "My mother's womb!" People in the seats quietly laugh. Tommy knowing, he is getting a rise out of this, winks at Felice, but Felice who is very upset for Tommy and his future mouths the words to him, "Please stop and take this seriously!" Tommy nods his head to her. "Okay for you!" The Prosecutor again turns to the judge, "Your honor?" The Judge is very serious to Tommy, "Mr. Cade, I don't like your attitude in my courtroom. Just answer the questions that are given to you... This is the last time... or else!" Tommy lifts his eyes very slowly, "I'm from Chi town, Illinois!" The prosecutor, angry at Tommy, "Thank you!" Then looks at the judge, "Is it true that you brutally assaulted that man pointing to Elliot Werner?" Tommy looks around, "Yeah, I did." The Prosecutor nodded his head, "What was your reason? Can you tell us in this courtroom?" Tommy stammers and very suppressed, looks down, "I'll tell you the truth, It was about four thirty in the morning, we both work late nights I told 5-0, I went to pick Felice up, thank god I heard her scream, in the ally way next to where she works and this dude here was going to try to rape my girl, she told me he kept hitting on her, and she didn't want anything to do with him. Anyway, I caught him just in time, and I slapped him around a little bit. Then my anger towards this turned into rage and I wanted to see his eyeballs pop out of his fuckin head! Then I really gave him a beating he'd never forget!" People in the courtroom are adjusted and can't believe Tommy said what he said. The judge's gavel hits his desk again, "Language, that strikes two!" Felice cries, "No, Tommy!" The Prosecutor continues to walk around then turns to Tommy, Mr. Cade, "is it true that you were thrown out of your house at the age of sixteen?" Tommy Looking down, "Yeah." The Prosecutor walking towards

Tommy, "Can you state why?" Tommy stammers a bit; "I didn't get along with my stepfather." looking at the judge, "Excuse my language." Looking at the judge, "HE WAS AN ASSHOLE!" The courtroom at this time is silent. The prosecutor looks at his notes, "HA... could you tell us why?" Tommy getting confused, "HE BEAT ME AND MY STEPMOTHER EVERY DAY, WITH A BELT! Until we both bled, then at the age of sixteen, he found out I could take care of myself, when he used his belt buckle for the last time." Tommy stands up and turns around and shows everyone the scars on his back due to the severe beatings he used to endure from Steve. "I then grabbed that same belt buckle from him and began beating the fuckin' shit out of him until he was so bloodied his face was unrecognizable for a month, he is so stubborn and so afraid of 5-0 he didn't even call them, that fuck job knows what he did to me and Renee, I was so raged out I thought I was going to kill him next time, but I didn't want to leave his daughter Nicole without a father so I thought it was best if I left!" Tommy kicks the chair and gets up and lunges at the prosecutor, "So you see FUCK JOB, that's what I've been through in my life!" The courtroom erupts in commotion. The Guards restrain Tommy. The Judge yells, "I've seen and heard enough. Bailiff, guards... take him away! One year in the state correctional facility." The guards put the cuffs back on Tommy and take him down the aisle of the courtroom. Felice screams and cries, and grabs onto Tommy's arm, "Tommy, Tommy, please don't take him, he doesn't deserve this!" Elliot Warner looks at Felice as she passes him, he stares at her winks and smiles at her, Felice looks at him and spits right in his face, Felice goes through the crowds of people to get to Tommy, the court guards try to hold Felice back, Tommy on the other hand has a worn out blank look on his face, looking straight ahead without saying a word.

Present Day, The Police Station....,

Felice thinking with tears in her eyes, this Police Station didn't make it make it easy for Tommy or me, I remember sleeping right over there I refused to leave until I knew for sure what was going to happen to him and where they were going to take him; He was locked up in that cell

for an additional twelve hours after the court judgment. I begged the officers to let me see him. At first they kept telling me no, but I stood my ground and there was one officer who just gave up and let me see him, So when I went down to cell block, When I saw him I felt so bad because he was sleeping on the floor like a dog, I just broke down, He woke up and looked at me, and ran over to the bars, and grabbed and kissed me and looked into my eyes and told me everything was going to be okay! Could you imagine what kind of man he was? He was the one locked up and being sent away somewhere and he's telling me everything was going to be okay! What a guy! She thinks for a moment, anyway he told me in a whisper for me to get in touch with Big Vic, and he would take care of all of this, and make sure he knew what was going on because if an E-6 member is missing more than Three days they're considered a deserter and were marked men and had a price on their head no matter who they were! I was scared to death to even talk to Big Vic, let alone telling him what had happened with Tommy. Tommy assured me it was all going to be okay! So, as hard as it was for me to leave this police station, I knew what I needed to do for Tommy's sake. It took me a day, but I finally got in touch with Vic and told him what was going on. I was scared to face him but relieved to know that he knew it was a funny feeling! Big Vic sat me down and told me that even though there were dozens of E-6 gang members, he respected Tommy the most! He pulled me close and told me to keep it a secret, even more than his own brother. Can you believe it? Vic told me Tommy would have to do some time because he didn't want 5-0 to start to look into them anymore than what they were already! At least the straight and narrow cops, anyway. He also told me he knew Tommy was stubborn as a mule. "HE LAUGHED ABOUT THAT" and wouldn't talk about anything of E-6 to anyone. That's why he had so much respect for him. Days passed, I haven't heard anything from Big Vic, and they sent Tommy to the correctional facility in downtown Chicago. I remember I worked every day and hopped a bus there every weekend to see him. Big Vic had so many connections that he got Tommy's sentence from a year to six months. I was so happy I couldn't believe it. Anyway, inside this facility Tommy had a counselor his name was Adam..........

TWENTY-SIX

Hidden Demons, Become Hidden Talents

Still the Present time..., Felice continues,

Every weekend, I remember visiting Tommy in the counseling facility, walking down a long hallway with the two guards, we had to pass cells with other inmates in there it was the lighting was very dim and creepy; I felt like the facility didn't want me there because I became a pain in the ass all the time I couldn't wait till Tommy was released and the guards tried to scare me and take me that route so it would deter me from coming back the next time and I'd leave Tommy be...., But they were so wrong. Nothing could stop me from seeing him. I was scared, but I tried not to show it. Those guys were sex pervs, that prayed on women when I walked by most of them they called me everything in the book and what they wanted to do to me, most of them haven't seen a woman in god knows how long, and the guards used to hit their nightsticks against the bars to calm them down......

To The Past...

The guards hitting their nightsticks against the bars, as the inmates are shouting at Felice 1st Guard shouts to the inmates, "Calm the hell down she is a woman not a piece of meat!" Felice looks at them as she walks past them, they now come up to a corner cell in which Tommy is, the cell is dark, he sleeps, the Guard stands on the side as Felice looks at Tommy and whispers to him, "Tommy! Tommy!" Tommy awakens, "FE?" Out of the dark corner, Tommy shows himself. He looks very scruffy from the week that she hasn't seen him, Felice very hurt, "Look what they have done to you!" Tommy has dark circles under his eyes from lack of

sleep. He reaches out his arms to her, and she touches his face. Tommy stammers, hanging on the cell bars, "What are you doing here Felice?" Felice trying to be strong, "What did you think, that I would just leave you here? I know the truth and what you did for me. And I'm going to fight to make them hear me. I'm never going to leave you, "EVER!" Tommy once again grabs Felice and kisses her... They look at one another, Tommy Looks at her, "Did you hear anything?" Felice nods her head, "Yes, now you need to listen to me, I know it's not you who opens up to too many people, but they have assigned you a counselor, He's supposedly very good, and you begin sessions with him tomorrow. His name is Adam. Listen, if you want to start our life together, you need to put everything you feel out to him, please Tommy, I love you! And it's killing me to see you in here like this." Tommy nods his head with tears in his eyes, "FOR US!"The guard walks back over to Felice, "Ms. are you done?" Felice looks down and then Tommy and Felice lock eyes, Felice nods her head, continuing to look at Tommy. To the guard, "YES!" Felice and the guard walk away. As Tommy helplessly watches them.

The Next Day.... Correctional Facility, hallway, Twelve forty-five p.m. Two Facility counselors talk about Tommy, one is a head counselor, and the other is counselor Adam Quinn, the head counselor briefs Adam on his subject who is Tommy, about his past, present, and future, Adam an ex-Gangbanger himself is very familiar with the lifestyle and is one of the top counselors in the state. Tommy is sitting in the room right outside where they are standing. Tommy sits in a chair with his back towards them. He looks out the window as the sunlight glares through. The Head Counselor pulled Adam close to him, "I'm telling you, Adam, this guy's a hard nut to crack. I have had everyone working with him ever since he got here two weeks ago. The guy doesn't want to eat, drink, or sleep. I know you were a gangbanger at one time, that's why I called you in here for this one. I have the utmost confidence in your work!" Adam nods his head, "Thank you very much, sir. I'll do my best, there's a certain way you have to talk to them. I'll see what I can do." The Head Counselor hands Adam Tommy's paperwork, "Okay if you have any problems call for a few

guards, He's strong as hell!" Adam nods his head, "I'll do that, sir." The Head Counselor walks away, "Good luck!" Adam looks in the doorway figuring out what would be the best way to approach Tommy, He puts his notebook under his arm and takes his glasses off and puts them in his pocket, then he walks into the room and stands next to Tommy. Tommy is silent and continues to stare straight out the window. Adam quickly throws his paperwork on the table like he is mad, "My name is Adam Quinn, I'm going to cut right through the bullshit, I was out on the fuckin streets like you since I was a kid joined a street gang at age eleven, sold narcotics, at age thirteen, by fifteen I was arrested dozens of times, until one day I had enough all of that shit, because I made a promise to my dying mother, I would straighten myself out, so I went back to school, graduated, worked shitty jobs, put myself through college and made sure I'd come out helping the world instead of being a fuckup in it! So, I don't care if you don't talk, but you damn better listen." Adam gets right in Tommy's face, "So if you want to take me out, take me out right here!" Tommy, with a stammer, "For one nobody wants to "Take you out" and two I already got the M.O. on you! So, what was your street name?" Adam looks out the window, "What?" Tommy smiles, "your street name?" Adam still looks out the window, "Ooh, I couldn't walk around with a name like Adam, so my name was A.Q." Tommy laughs, "A...Q? You must have been looking tough with your pink slippers and pink teddy bear on the corner waiting for your mommy, with your thumb in your mouth!" Adam turns around, and smiles, "OOH... I see where this is going, I can't make you believe me, but it's all true, listen we're not here for me, I'm through with all of that shit. I found my way out! I heard you went through four counselors in two weeks, and they all gave up on you. I was up for days looking at your file and I know I can help you out. If you want to change, get through your problems, I'm a former gangbanger that will listen!" Tommy looked at Adam, "I told ya, I know what you're about, I'll never snitch on my crew, you will have to torture and threaten to kill me before I do that! But I do need help with my personal issues that have plagued me all my life, and I need a new direction." Adam pulls up a chair and sits next to Tommy. "All bullshit aside, I promise you Tommy, I can definitely help you with

your personal problems, and I won't ever mention the crew you're with. I JUST WANT TO HELP YOU! all you need to do is open up!" Tommy looks out the window, "You know, as I get older, I feel selfish because you hear it all the time about families, kids not getting along with their parents and all that shit. It's all over the place, right? But nobody knows the individual, right? Everyone handles things differently. Someone may go into their room and cry. I see it as a threat and I want to bust someone's face open because I know how it feels to have someone tell you every day that you are worthless, and not about that life, but always getting a beating for nothing, because you were not really their kid, getting played mind games with starving them. Then when the motherfucker came home from his truck job for a few days beat me until I bled, He threatened Renee all the time, and she took beatings for me too! He sweet-talked her, she got pregnant they had a kid, Nicole, she's innocent in all of this by the way, I hold no grudges with her at all! But this motherfucker Steve made a complete three sixty, Renee now stuck it out with him, and Nicole is the apple of his eye, and I have fuckin scars on half my body because of his abuse. Now the only person I trust in my fuckin' life is Felice!" Adam shaking his head, "I feel ya, man! We're going to work all this out for you!" Adam puts a notebook and pen in front of Tommy, "Every night I want you to mark down your thoughts and ideas in this pad, and we will go over it the next day Ok! Remember anything and everything that bothers you. But I have to tell you, I need you to really open up!" Tommy nods his head.

Felice in the present....,

It was the craziest thing, because Tommy was actually taking Adam's advice and writing down everything, he could think of all of his thoughts and problems. Tommy didn't trust anybody, he didn't let anyone in his mind, that's how good Adam Quinn was, someone who actually cared for other human beings and Tommy saw right through him and trusted almost everything that Adam taught him. And I'm telling you, "At that time as a young counselor I've learned tons from him also!" Felice looked out the window, while Tommy was away, I spent much time with Adam's wife

Sarah, and their kids too. They treated and took me in like I was family, and sometimes I'd babysit for them so they could go out! Adam repaid me by teaching me all he knew about counseling troubled kids and adults, also Adam arranged for me to spend nights at the facility with Tommy. I was so happy just to be with Tommy, I didn't care where we were as long as we were together, that's all I could have ever wanted! Adam knew Tommy did what he did in self-defense that night and why he did it, so he was working tooth and nail to get him out quicker! But every time he asked the judge to make an appeal for him, it was declined. At that time, I had lost all my respect in the justice system, again I said to myself, "What justice system?" But even though we had Adam working the hardest he could for us, not a day went by that Tommy was in there that I didn't worry that the courts judge was going to find out that the E-6 Thunder wasn't just some hustling gangbangers, that robbed and stole from the innocent, but were a street gang ready to stand up for what is right, and help the innocent, and were trying to go global and take back the streets everywhere for everyone! But they were vigilantes, and they did kill a number of lowlifes. I thought if the judge found out that Tommy was in the forefront at most times, he would throw the key away for Tommy and I would never see him again! But Tommy was so brilliant he never gave up an ounce of info to anyone! Not even Adam!

But even though Adam was getting through Tommy's surface problems Adam had a much difficult time with the inner demons Tommy struggled with, it took months before Tommy would open up about these things, but when he did even Adam had to dig deeper in himself, to help Tommy, It was confidential but Adam and I talked about it, off the record because he knew I was the closest to Tommy! There was one instance where Tommy opened up so much to Adam that all hell broke loose. He told me he could almost see Tommy's soul! Adam was so frightened he told me he was questioning himself on if he wanted to continue Tommy's therapy or not!

Back to the past....,

In the one-on-one counseling room, Tommy sits in the room as Adam stands outside talking to the head counselor, Adam looking in the room at Tommy, "I'm really getting through to him, but no lie he's one of the toughest I had so far, let's walk sir because I don't want him to hear me! He's brilliant. He reads you like a book. Yes, he could be a danger, but he has a vulnerable side which makes him a good guy! Thank God! And his girlfriend Felice sees something very special in him too, that's why she feels so connected to him. Honestly, they are two extraordinary people!" The head counselor nods his head, "Adam, you are doing a fine job, after Cade, I want you on staff here full time, I will match and pay you double what the other facility is paying you!" Adam happy, "Thank you Sir, I appreciate that! And if it's not too much to ask for, I would like Felice Levito to work as my part-time assistant. She has a counseling job, but I can use her. She's brilliant!" The Head Counselor nods his head, "Okay, we will talk about it, just get everything out of Cade, and see if he is able to function in the real world!"

The Head Counselor walks away down the hall as Adam is a bit apprehensive and takes a deep breath and walks into the room, Tommy is still sitting there staring out the window. Adam walks over to Tommy, "Hey Tommy, what's going on? How was your weekend? Did you write anything down in the book I gave you?" Tommy sullen, "Yeah, but I'm not ready to show anyone yet!" Adam nods his head, "Okay! No rush whenever you want! Any inmates giving you any trouble? No..., they're a bunch of pussies! They know better than to touch me!" Adam tries not to stir him up, "I feel ya' man! Anyway, today I want to get to the core of your problems. Everybody has a core, the deeper stuff. I know it's hard for you to open up and all. It's just me and you, man, I promise! No recorders, just me and you talking about what makes you tick, bro! You trust me, don't you!" Tommy smiles and nods his head, "Yeah! But if I didn't, I'd have to hurt you severely!" Adam is still reluctant, but knows he has a job to do. "Please don't I have a family to look after and support!" Tommy laughs,

"Just fuckin with ya!" and then Tommy gets serious, and looks down to the ground, "What blows my fuckin mind, is this world and the people in it! Child predators, rapists, murderers who walk the streets looking for their next victim! This is the shit that keeps me up at night and scares me! I'm not stupid, I know there must be a balance of good and evil in the world, but it always seems that evil wins? And the parents of these victims have to struggle through it all without their loved ones that they cherish most! Justice doesn't prevail for the good at times, then at the end of a person's life, what good is it for? What does it all mean? Sometimes I feel like I'm just one person, But I know I can make a difference in another person's life for the better. It's not about money or power, it's about protecting the ones you love, and the ones that are less fortunate, the innocent young and old alike! But I feel if I don't tell all that's on my mind, or like getting those fuckin scumbags off the streets, and I have kids one day and when I die, WHAT WILL HAPPEN TO THEM? Look at the role models, in all walks of life, Celebrities, Police, Churches, Teachers, Politicians, they're the worst! No wonder kids today are all fucked up." "Do AS I SAY, DON'T DO AS I DO! or when a kid does follow these supposed role models, they teach the kids the wrong things and then a good parent is stuck to clean up the mess, and what I mean when I say a good parent one who takes time to do the right thing and listen to their kids and try to raise them right! I know when I have kids. If I have them one day, I will try to do what I can to end the corruptive ways of people! You know when you're a child, your parents teach you one thing they try to teach and instill these moral values, something I was never taught, but I've seen a lot of it around, and it's all good, until you become a young adult and then a teen you go out into this fucked up world we live in and then, all those morals go into the garbage can for some reason!" "So then young motherfuckers say what's the sense of being good? I'll rob and steal, or when they don't get their way, they harm another human being. Then they become another statistic!" "What a world we live in, huh? So that's what's always on my fuckin mind, What I can do to improve this fucked up world we live in. This cesspool we call life!" Adam is completely dumbfounded by what Tommy

has said for a moment and has tears in his eyes and nods his head, "I got you Tommy! I understand you now!"

TWENTY-SEVEN

Out Of Darkness Comes Light

That same day..., One forty-five p.m. The counselor lunchroom,

Adam sits in the lunchroom with a fellow co-worker counselor named Cindy, Adam goes over Tommy's reports with her and is still mesmerized over there session earlier that morning, Adam almost in tears talks heartfelt to her, Adam looking over his paperwork, "Cindy, you know me pretty good right and you trust me?" Cindy Nods her head, "Adam you're one of my mentors in this field of course!" Adam moves closer to her, "I've never seen anything like this case 'Tommy Cade!' If I could even call it that anymore? I'm almost spooked! This guy has seen inside my frigging soul. And it's all heartfelt! It was all true! Mark my words, that guy is filled with something great! I know this might all sound corny and all, but not just for himself or people around him, but it's like for all of mankind or something? This guy feels the way others in power should feel but choose to ignore it!" Cindy takes a sip of her drink. "Hey, listen Adam, I can tell this hit you very hard, just keep working with him and bring his case up to see what you can do to get him out of here if you feel that strongly about it I know if anyone can do it, it's you!" Adam nods his head.

Same day..., Six o'clock p.m., inmates at dinnertime,

Adam walks into the cafeteria area, to make sure, Tommy is at the tables eating dinner, with the other inmates at the start of dinnertime, Adam walks passed him, but making sure that Tommy doesn't see him, Adam now walks past a row of cells and right to Tommy's room. Adam keeps the lights out and brings a flashlight and works fast, going through Tommy's belongings. Knowing he can get into serious trouble for doing this, he

works quickly and very efficiently. Adam comes across a rather large suitcase of Tommy's opens it and at first see's clothes on top, he hears shuffling outside of the cells and stops and checks it out, sweat pours off of his brow, and goes back to what he is doing, he puts the clothes aside and comes across newspaper articles about E-6 Thunder and their heroic efforts of vigilantism all around Chicago and now spreading to different parts of the country, Adam now in shock shakes his head, to himself, "Ooh shit' E-6 Thunder, I've heard of these guys, they don't play!" Up until this point Adam knew Tommy was in a street gang but did not know he was affiliated with E-6 Thunder, because Tommy never let up on who he was with. And says to himself, "Now it all makes sense! You go Tommy! and E-6!" Continuing to work as fast as he can, he begins to take pictures of all the articles with his iPhone and after he is done, he puts his phone back into his pocket. Now as he begins to put the clothes back into the suitcase, he comes across the notebook he had given Tommy months before, Adam with his flashlight picks it up and goes through the book and realized that Tommy has written a full-length screenplay entitled, "ALL IS FORGIVEN A "NEW DAWNING" IN LIFE." Adam with tears, "I fuckin knew it! Yes Tommy! I got your back! Adam now shifts through many of the pages, this sounds incredible! Now I know I can help you, Tommy!" Once again very impressed with what he sees Tommy has written, he takes out his iPhone and takes pictures not to share just yet, but he needs to break the news gently to Tommy without him getting upset that he looked through his belongings without his consent. Adam now quickly puts all of the things, including the screenplay, back into the suitcase and rushes out of the room.

That same night eleven fifty p.m......,

Adam on his way home is looking in his iPhone still completely in awe about what Tommy has written, as he is driving decides to call Felice, Adam dials his phone, Felice's voicemail picks up, with a bit of urgency in his voice, "Yeah, Felice, this is Adam Quinn! Can you please come down to the facility tomorrow? It's about Tommy, nothing bad but very serious,

this is for his future! Thanks, have a good night!" He puts his phone down and drives off.

The very next day…, at nine a.m. Felice's consultation with Adam,

Felice sits in Adam's office waiting for him as he is in the next room looking through his paperwork on Tommy. Felice hears him on the phone with someone. Unknown to her at this time, this is Adam's movie producer friend. Adam has told him all about Tommy and the screenplay that he had written. Adam on the phone to his friend, "Ok! I will have it out to you as soon as we clean it up! But I still need his consent and I don't know how hard this is going to be! Ok? I will get back to you asap! yep!" Adam hangs up his phone and walks out to Felice. Adam looked very disheveled. "Hey Felice, I'm sorry to make you wait, I was on the phone with a longtime friend!" Felice looking at him, "That's ok!" Adam rushes around looking for paperwork on his desk, "And the way I look, I haven't slept for two days!" Felice senses something but pauses for a moment and begins to tear up, and knows what Adam is thinking before he even gets a chance to say anything, "OOH, MY GOD! You've seen the same thing I see in Tommy? He's not like everyone else, right?" Adam, at this time stops dead in his tracks, "HE'S OF SPECIAL QUALITY! I don't know how to describe him. He's in a class by himself." Felice in tears, "On a higher level, just what I've been saying all my life! He doesn't focus on the trivial things most of us focus on." Adam finishes the sentence, "HE'S ONE OF A KIND!" He whispers, "I broke so many rules here Felice, if anyone ever found out, I could lose my counseling license for life, and they could put me in prison forever! I know what set Tommy is with so you don't need to hide it anymore, and between me and you I support them a billion percent there should be more like them this world wouldn't be, excuse my language "FUCKED UP," I promise to you I will take this to the grave, and I know that I shouldn't have but as Tommy and the other inmates had dinner last night I went into Tommy's room and searched through his duffle bag and found this!" Adam throws the screenplay on the desk in front of Felice! She picks it up and looks at it. Adam goes on,

"A full length screenplay! I made a copy, it's brilliant! Now I know you can sue me for everything that I own, for what I've done, but when I talked to him yesterday something made me look at him deeper, so when he was eating dinner last night I went to his room and saw this! And this morning when the inmates were having breakfast I went back to the room and made a copy!" Felice looks at Adam, "I don't know what to say? I should be pissed off at you for doing this? But happy at the same time, for Tommy's sake. But this doesn't surprise me at all. I always knew what Tommy was all about." Adam sits next to her. "Now listen, I have a very good friend. He does low to mid budget movies, and he is looking for his next big breakout film, and I know we have a winner here! But if Tommy finds out what I've done, I may not live to see my children grow up! Anyway, I gave him this notepad when I first met him to write down his thoughts and each time, I saw him I asked for this book, and he was apprehensive of showing me and I let it go until I felt he was comfortable in doing so and he came up with this masterpiece! I'm telling you if this is produced right, which it will be because my friend is a brilliant filmmaker, THIS WILL BE A BLOCKBUSTER! A movie with heart and feeling, something you don't see anymore! Please Felice, can you help me? Help Tommy?" Felice nods her head, thinking how she's going to break it to him, "It's not going to be easy, but It needs to be done for Tommy's sake!" Adam replied, "You too are an extraordinary person Felice, I'm going to work like hell in the next few days on getting Tommy out of here, also and hatch a plan to get him to see his mother and stepfather too." Felice replies, "I trust you Adam" nodding her head.

Later that night......, Adam has arranged for Felice to spend the night at the facility with Tommy, in a private room away from the other Inmates, The two just got done having sex on the floor and Tommy kisses Felice with passion, Tommy looking into Felice's eyes, "I love you!" Felice shivering, "I love you too, forever and always!" Tommy now gets up off of her, and grabs his shirt that is on the bed, Felice looks at him and covers herself up. As Tommy sits on the bed, putting his boots on. Felice feels now is the right time to tell him what Adam was up to, and she covers herself

once again and crawls up to Tommy and kneels in front of him. Felice is a bit apprehensive but begins to tell all, "I talked to Adam today and he is also taken by you, Tommy! He sees in you what I've always seen in you." Tommy looking down, "Yeah? When did he say I was getting out of here?" Felice Smiles, "Sooner than you think! Now listen Tommy, you need to listen to me very carefully, like I said, Adam sees something in you that he has never seen in anyone before, and he has worked with hundreds of people! He found it..." Tommy looks at Felice, "Found what?" Felice softly, "The movie you've written!" Tommy is very angry, "What?" Tommy takes a table, picks it up and throws it against the wall and smashes it, and rushes over to Felice, "What the fuck, Fe?" Felice, quite shaken, backs off for a moment. Tommy shouts, "What? he just walked in here and looked at my shit? I should beat his mother fuckin' ass! That was for me to show him when I was ready!" Felice replies, "Tommy calm down and just listen to me, he knew, and I knew it was totally wrong for what he did, trust me when I found out I was pissed too but he was so intrigued by you he needed to know more about you that's all! You've really impressed him! So much, in fact, he has some movie producer and filmmaker friends interested in it also, you've done it. Tommy, put your anger away and look towards your future! Our future, don't you want to spend the rest of our lives together like we've always talked about or not!" Tommy calms down a bit, "Of course!" Felice moves closer to him, "Ok, then just trust me, I have your back, I wouldn't do anything to hurt you!" Tommy once again grabs Felice and kisses her.

TWENTY-EIGHT

Tommy's Way Out

A few days pass, Tommy sits in the library of the facility, at a table reading with handcuffs on, with a guard standing at his side. Walking up at the door is Felice with Adam, who is still reluctant to go in and talk to him about what he did, Felice assures Adam that everything is okay, and Tommy is understanding why he did it.

Felice nudges Adam's arm, "Just go and talk to him, Adam! He's ok! Tommy knows this is big for him!" Adam nods his head, "Okay!" And slowly begins to walk over to him, Tommy already knows that he is going to mess with him a bit, smirks, Adam walks up to him, with a lump in his throat, "Tommy, can I talk to you for a sec?" Tommy, at first is unresponsive, Adam puts Tommy's completed screenplay in front of him. Adam is nervous, "It's all in proper format which Felice helped me with. Please forgive me Tommy for what I've done here, but this points to the screenplay, but this points to Tommy, you are going to be somebody!" Tommy laughs, "I am already somebody, I'm a human being, ain't I?" Adam gets his humor and laughs, "You know what I'm talking about! Pick up the screenplay, this and your mind! You have the power to change people. I know that Felice already told you that I have a friend that is a producer and filmmaker, and he was looking for the next big thing, And I sent him a copy of this, and he was floored by it. This dude is so into it he already has the actors to portray the roles. The only thing that's stopping him is the funding of the money to produce it! But don't worry about that yet. He's getting it covered, you've just stepped in a one in a million-crap shoot and won the bet! I want to be there when you make it, you deserve it!"

Tommy raises his wrists, "I can't do anything until I get these frigging things off!" Felice walks over to them and smiles, Adam smiles, "Guard! You can take off the cuffs now!" Felice hugs Tommy. Now Tommy turns around free of the handcuffs and looks at Felice after years of feeling like a nobody, now has tears of happiness deep within him. Adam looks at Tommy, very happy for him, "And you get out of here tomorrow morning!" Tommy gets up very happily, hugs Felice and says softly to her, "I'm out of here!"

Later that same night...,

Tommy and Felice are in his cell room packing up his things, standing next to one another, Felice looking at Tommy. Felice folding clothes, "Tommy, let me ask you a question? Why didn't you ever tell me you write this good?" Tommy looking in his bag, "You never asked! You know you must have millions of dollars' worth of material here!" Tommy continues to look in his bag, "Maybe. We'll see if Adam comes through like he said." Felice stands up, "He will!" Felice smiles, but thinking of Tommy, "Yeah, now maybe you could become a king like you said you wanted to become." Hesitating a bit like she doesn't want to say it, "With all your women around you!" Tommy raises his head and slowly shakes it, puts his hand in her hand and gets on one knee, looking up at her, "Felice, I had a lot of time to think in here and I would, like to make you my wife, because I want to spend the rest of my life with you!" Felice looks at Tommy as her eyes fill up with tears. Felice, teary-eyed, "Oh Tommy!" Tommy continues to hold on to her hand. "I know sometimes it's hard to tell what I'm thinking, but I want you to stand by my side forever! I'm sorry I don't have a ring for you, I'll get one asap!" Felice cries looking at him, "Forget the ring! Of course, I'll marry you! But if we bring kids into this world one day, I'll need to know you will be there with me! I really wish you would back off with some not all the things E-6 does, I know you can handle yourself Tommy. But what if something happens to you? What will I do without you?" Tommy nods his head, Felice looks straight into his eyes, "But I will, I want to stand by your side forever! I've always loved you, Tommy!"

Tommy gets up off his knee and they kiss one another passionately.

The day of Tommy's release…, Twelve Noon, The front of the facility, It's a bright sunny day, Adam made a special visit on his day off, to see Tommy and Felice out, Adam is there also with his wife who has been very close to both of them, Adam walks with Felice as Tommy walks with a guard and Adam's wife in the foreground. Adam happy walking with his hands in his pockets, "So that's great." Tommy popped the question, "to you huh?" In a joking way, "And you said yes?.... Great! I wish you all the best!" Felice smiles, "This is not goodbye or anything, You guys are a part of our family now, we appreciate everything that you've done for us! We owe you our lives!" Adam smiles, "you guys are very special to us too. Listen, get settled in when you guys get home in about a month, give me a call, and if you're interested, I talked to the head counselor here, I can use you to work under me as my apprentice! I think you have a talent for counseling and I can work with you, get you in the big leagues and make more money than where you're at!" Felice stops for a moment and is overjoyed, and hugs Adam, "Ooh my god Adam that's great! I'm definitely going to take it, what can I say!" Adam laughs, "Don't thank me it's all you I can use you!" Adam's wife comes over to Felice and smiles as Felice tells her the good news, Adam to his wife and Felice, "I just got to talk to Tommy alone for a sec, ok?" Adam looks to the guard, "Were ok, Thank you!" The guard walks away. The two men walk away from the ladies Adam checks to see if anyone else is around or if he is in a range of camera's and whispers to Tommy, "You have come a long way Tommy, I'm proud of you, Very direct to him, You go out to those streets and protect those innocent, people You show those criminal "Mother Fuckers!", what E-6 is made of! I'm all for what you guys are doing out there and what you guys stand for! And when this screenplay gets produced, you're going to become a legend!" Tommy just looks at Adam, nods his head, and gives him a fist pound! "Adam was down, right?" Tommy nods his head. Tommy now knows Adam is on the same page as he is. Then they walk back to the ladies.

Present day... Police station Felice stares out the window,

Tommy was released finally! Just a little after four months in the facility, Tommy made sure everything was cleared with Big Vic and Gatch, so they knew he wasn't running from them or anything when they heard we were getting married. They set us up for a three-night stay in Las Vegas; they paid for everything for us! They were the best! That was Big Vic's way of telling Tommy how much he appreciated him or not talking about anything that had to do with E-6 business!! We were married right in the heart of Vegas, in this little chapel, Tommy made me pick out anything that I wanted, then we went back to the hotel and stood there the whole day and night! We had a great time there! Then when we came back, about two weeks later is when I received a call from Adam, I met the head counselor again, but this time it was on a whole different level, to work with and counsel the inmates there and I have to tell you it was a relief this time it wasn't Tommy on that end! And Tommy continued to work two jobs for us, "What a guy"! We couldn't wait to hear something back from Adam's producer friend to get Tommy started on his better direction! Also, Adam kept urging me to contact and get information on where Steve and Renee were so Tommy could meet with them for closure, He felt if Tommy could just talk about the things that has plagued him all of his life, he could put these things to rest since now Tommy was an adult now and maybe put the past to rest for good! And I supported him one hundred percent with E-6 Thunder, but I constantly worried about its consequences. That's why I wanted him to back away a bit without becoming a nagging wife! But he told me he was in too deep!

TWENTY-NINE

Settling an Unsettled score

Location: The Diner where Felice used to work, Time One a.m.

Two days after Tommy is back from Las Vegas... Tommy and Big Vic sit in Big Vic's car. Tommy is in the driver's seat. Tommy got word from an E-6 crew member that Elliot Warner was in the area, and around the diner asking about Felice and harassing other waitresses that work there constantly. Tommy and Big Vic are patient as they wait for him to exit the diner, both men are dressed in their gang colors black and white with a white and black bandana covering their faces, the car windows are tinted so passing police cars are oblivious to the two inside the car. Tommy gets his gun ready and a leather belt, looking intently in the diner, "Come on motherfucker, show yourself!" Big Vic smiles also looking intently, "Ooh he'll be out, or we'll go in there to get him, that fucker must be on something, look at him chasing that waitress around, He deserves everything he's going to get!" Tommy nodding his head, "I'm going to rip out his fuckin organs." (A cop car passes), "5-0 Lay low!" The two men duck, Big Vic Laughs, "Donut run!" Tommy, "Yeah!" A while goes by.

A half hour later...., The cook, the same one who helped out Felice a time ago chases Elliot Werner out of the diner again, the cook screams at him, "FOR THE LAST TIME LEAVE THE FUCKIN' WAITRESSES ALONE DAMNIT, THEIR WORKING HERE!" Now as Elliot walks away, he curses at the cook, "Yeah, Yeah, I'm horny I want to get laid! Is there any harm in that?" The cook shouts back, "Go downtown, and get yourself a hooker then if you're that hard up!" Elliot screams back, "Fuck you" and throws a bottle at him and walks away! The cook then ducks the thrown bottle and shouts, "KEEP WALKING!" Now Elliot turns and walks away. The cook

shakes his head and walks back into the diner, and says to himself, "I don't know what I'm going to do!" and shuts the door behind him. Tommy and Big Vic adjust their bandanas and slowly Tommy drives, following an unsuspecting Elliot, Big Vic like a dog stalking its prey, "He's headed for the bus station!" As Elliot walks, he harasses some teenage girls, asking them questions, "Hey, do you want a date for tonight?" The one girl turns around and replies, "Watch it old man, we're only Fifteen!" Elliot then replies, and laughs, "Hey that's old enough for me!" The two girls run away, Elliot Shouts Back, "I HAVE A BIG ONE!" Tommy pissed off, "That motherfucker!" Big Vic replies, "Turn this car around, this fucker has to go!" Tommy turns the car around, and both get out right in front of Elliot and grab him. Big Vic takes his head and smashes it into the car window, Tommy begins kicking him relentlessly. Elliot screams, Tommy now begins to choke the life out of Elliot and shouts, "FIFTEEN-YEAR-OLD KIDS? YOU FUCKIN PIECE OF GARBAGE!" Big Vic opens the back door of the car and throws Elliot inside by his hair and begins to choke the life out of him Tommy runs to the front of the driver's side and pulls away with the tires screeching, Big Vic Shouts to Tommy, "YOU KNOW WHERE TO TAKE HIM!" Elliot gasping for air pleads to them to stop! Big Vic Shouts to him, "SHUT THE FUCK UP! YOU'RE GOING TO MEET YOUR MAKER NOW... THE DEVIL!" Tommy now pulls into a remote place an abandoned apartment complex that had a huge fire years earlier, Big Vic opens the back door and kicks Elliot out of the car, he falls to the ground, Tommy runs over to him, and bends down, and screams at him, "DO YOU HAVE KIDS?" Elliot crying and out of breath and very bloodied doesn't respond at first, An Irate Tommy shouts again grabbing him by his hair, "MOTHER FUCKER! DO... YOU... HAVE... KIDS?" "Yes, two girls ages four and six, but I don't see them anymore, since I left my wife." Big Vic takes out a piece of paper, "It doesn't matter anyway, we already have your M.O.! Right heart attack and assault on dozens of females in the Chicago area. You're from fuckin Cali. Why don't you stay their bitch?" "Especially young waitresses. What is it you get off on that or something, huh? You freak!" Tommy spits on him, "You fuckin scum of the earth!" Big Vic kicks him in the head, "what do you think we're going to do let you go free and maybe

if you get caught being a perv the cops will pick you up off the street you will do a little jail time and slap you on the wrist, and you'll be out doing this shit all over again? Your fate ends tonight motherfucker, one by one scum like you are done!" Tommy and Big Vic begin to strip Elliot of his clothes, Tommy now takes out his blade and tags Elliot's body with the knife carving E-6 into it, and he screams for mercy! Tommy Shouts "GOD AIN'T GONNA HELP YOU BITCH!" Big Vic replies, "But the Devil might! Your kids will probably be better off without you anyway!" Tommy and Big Vic begin to hogtie Elliot and drag him over to the corner of the building Elliot screams and Irate Tommy once again gets right in his face and takes off his bandana, Elliot looks at him. Tommy, with vengeance in his eyes and soul, "I WANT THIS TO BE THE LAST FACE YOU SEE ON THIS FUCKIN' EARTH! E-6 THUNDER MOTHER FUCKER!" With Big Vic sitting on Elliot's back, choking him, Tommy opens his mouth and solves a gun inside and blows Elliot's brains all over the place. Tommy and Big Vic get up, and kick Elliot's lifeless body, and then stop what they are doing, and proceed to walk away, Big Vic, with blood all over him, "He won't be bothering anyone else anymore, That piece of trash! Let 5-0 find him!"

Days later....., On the news and newsstands everywhere, is the report of The California businessman with a long history of sexual assaults against many young women in the Chicago area Elliot Werner, succumbed to a vigilante style demise! Felice doing grocery shopping spots this on the front page of the newspaper. At the checkout buys the paper and with the rest of her groceries and walks out the store. The word out on the Chicago streets is that E-6 Thunder are responsible, but there are so many of them, which ones? The authorities are at a standstill at this time, and don't know who to blame.

THIRTY

Felice's simpler times

Weeks after the Elliot Werner incident...,

The hype about the story is still in full effect all around. Felice and Tommy are out to dinner with Ashlie and her boyfriend, all of them are laughing and joking around, in this restaurant there is a big screen T.V. The local news comes on and immediately begins to talk about the Elliot Werner incident. The four-stop laughing for a moment, and look at one another, Tommy and Felice's eyes lock on one another. Ashlie and her boyfriend know Tommy is affiliated with E-6 thunder, but have no idea that it was Tommy who killed Elliot Werner and don't say a word about anything. The newscaster moves on to the next story, and Tommy picks up the conversation he was having with Ashlie and her boyfriend.

Felice's mind begins to drift back into the past at her fifth birthday party back in Belleville, NJ. It's a very bright sunny afternoon; many friends and family members are sitting in the backyard laughing and playing games with the other children. As Felice's father Frank mans the grill with a chef like manner, singing his favorite song that plays on the radio as he cooks the food, making others join in with him as they sing along and laugh. This is just a once in a lifetime, an ideal day for such an impressionable child like Felice. She sits at the picnic table with her aunt and uncle, who hug her tightly and laugh with her. Felice looks around in amazement, knowing this is all for her. Felice's mom Sandy announces that it is time for a birthday cake. Felice smiles and looks to the side and out of the bright sunlight around the corner of the house comes a rambunctious Tommy with a paper airplane in his hand shouting "I want cake!" "Save me some cake!" As Renee picks him up kissing him and hugging him and

brings him over to the table and sits him down next to Felice, Sandy now begins to light the candles on the cake and everyone begins to sing happy birthday to her and a young Tommy puts his arm around her shoulder, and Felice turns and smiles at him. And everyone finishes the happy birthday song and laughs, having a great time, Sandy kisses Felice and smiles, "Happy birthday my sweety! Now make a wish and blow out the candles, and don't tell anyone your wish!" Tommy grabs her hand and Felice blows out the candles on the cake. Everyone claps, gathering around her, people at the party note how cute Felice and Tommy are together, Renee hugs Tommy and smiles, Tommy gives Felice a good luck kiss! Tommy, not shy at all, does so and says to her, "Happy birthday, Felice!" Like everyone, Ooh's and Ahh's about them both. Frank laughs and jokes, "Hey Tommy, are you going to marry my daughter one day?" Tommy, who is not in the least bit shy, "Yes Sir, we're going to live in a big house and everything! Right Felice?" Felice is quite shy but smiles, "Yep! Just me and you!" Again, people can't believe the connection both children have for one another. At this time Steve, just returning from work, comes through the gate of the backyard, looking very pissed off and ready to take his frustrations out on Renee and Tommy. Steve, not worrying about who's there, yells for Renee to get up and leave at that moment. Now Frank sees what is happening and walks over to Steve, intervening on what he is about to do, Frank very direct, "NOT TODAY, IT'S MY DAUGHTERS BIRTHDAY!" It seems for this moment Steve has somewhat of a heart and understands, Frank puts his arm around Steve, "Come on I'll get you a beer!" and they walk past Renee and Tommy as they do Steve points and mouths the words to both of them, "You two are in for it later that I promise you that." Renee, Sandy, Tommy and Felice, all see him doing this. Renee hugs Tommy tightly, then looks at Sandy.

Nighttime falls..., That same night, nine forty-five p.m.

Arguing ensues in the Cade household as Felice sheds tears for her friend Tommy as she looks out her bedroom window at Tommy's house, she sees silhouettes of Steve beating Tommy and Renee, shouting vulgarities

at them both. Everyone in the neighborhood knows what goes on inside the house, but nobody involves themselves because they know Steve and his violent past. Felice cries as she gets under her blankets and covers her ears and cries herself to sleep.

Back to the present day,

The restaurant, with Tommy talking to her friends, and without him noticing, Felice with a tear in her eye, nods her head, and smiles at Tommy feeling very settled and a strong connection with him, knowing this is where she wants to and needs to be.

Later that same night...,

At home Tommy and Felice have passionate sex. Afterward, as they lay in bed together, they talk about their plans for the future. Tommy looking at Felice, "You know Fe, You deserve everything I'm going to buy you a ring first!" Felice jokes, "Oh, yeah I'll believe it when I see it!" Tommy, "come on, you know I'm working on it!" Felice replies and smiles. "I know just busting ya!" Tommy nods his head and smiles back, "And if this shit ever works out with Adam, I'm going to buy you the biggest frigging house you've ever seen!" Felice replies, "Ahh Tommy you know I'm not like that, just being with you is all I've ever wanted! We can really have a great life together, and I know you are going to be successful in anything you do!" Tommy again kisses Felice with so much passion.

Tommy sits up on the edge of the bed. He has many tattoos dedicated to E-6 Thunder on his back and arms, as Felice rubs the back of his arm she sees and feels a branding and letters on the back of his right arm, that are (E-6) (T) (G) (R) THE (Y) AND (O) FOR (L) as Felice touches down his arm, she asks "What does this branding mean? And what did you have to do to join? If you can't tell me, it's okay!" Tommy, "I'll tell you, it doesn't matter, but it doesn't leave this house!" Felice a little reluctant but curious to hear, "Maybe you shouldn't?" Tommy cuts her off and just

begins to talk, "E-6 (T) Thunder, (G) Guardians (R) Reppin The (I) Innocent (Y) Young And The (O) Old for (L) Life..........., I got brutally jumped in by six members, reppin E-6, (Tommy has flashbacks of his jump in) First they make sure to break some ribs, then they beat you so bad to see how much pain you can endure for two days straight, they gag your mouth and hang you upside down, in a pitch black room, and beat you with a belt, spitting on you, only giving you sips of water every few hours. And the last thing they do to you as you hand upside down is take a branding iron and burn these letters into you if anyone as much as makes a sound while they do this to you, they will not even consider you and that's all for nothing! And while you are a member of E-6 and you become disloyal to this brand for any reason, and they need to go, meaning die, We need to cut this out of them no questions! This showing your loyalty to E-6 and the innocent we protect! It's a brotherhood like no other, but just knowing the outcome of all that torture you endure means you're going to help others "the innocent" in the process the torture doesn't matter, to most of E-6, the ones that are loyal, that's worth all the money in the world!" Felice is amazed at what Tommy has just told her, Felice with tears, "Oh my god Tommy!" Tommy now gets up from the bed and says, "I have a meeting with Big Vic and Gatch in forty-five!"

THIRTY-ONE

A long hard decision becomes reality

At the present time...., The police station,

Felice hits the desk with her fist and shakes her head, "till this day I could not believe what Tommy had told me on how he joined E-6 and what he needed to endure to get in!" Shaking her head, "If I thought Tommy had so much integrity about things around him before, they at that time just magnified a thousand times over after I heard him tell me that! All of E-6, they were BADASS all the way!!" I will say it again, "Who do you know who would put their own lives on the line for others? For nothing, NOT A DIME!! It takes a special breed of people to do that! And also laying low and not taking any recognition for their services?" thinks and shakes her head and takes a short pause, "but getting back to Tommy and all the seemingly good fortune heading our way, that we were so desperately waiting for, It took a lot of doing but Tommy trusted me completely in me now and he knew I would never hurt him so I convinced him to contact Steve and Renee and I knew it was time for him to make peace with his troubled past, and make a decision and reach out to them but we were both unsure on how to approach it." We searched relentlessly online for their whereabouts; Tommy was shocked to find out they had never left New Jersey. They moved from Belleville to the next town over in Nutley on Grant Ave, in a big beautiful yellow house! I could tell without him even telling me, He was both excited and reluctant about seeing them again. He really wanted to see Nicole but was afraid that she wouldn't remember who he was, He told me that he was sort of scared if she actually forgot! And I told him that "That would be impossible!" Then about Steve, I told him to be the bigger man and show him what kind of man you've become! And if he didn't accept him, it really doesn't matter, I

told him you're a man now with your own ideals and goals! You're beyond that abuse he had dished out and as for Renee, he knew she would always accept him because he knew she had a bond with her, and she would always love him. You know Tommy was a big guy. A lot of people loved and respected him, but when it came to those three people in his life, it was like he was a frightened little child, to me, it was heart wrenching to watch! It sounds weird, but they were like his kryptonite that brought him to his knees, without him knowing it I applied my own counseling skills to walk him through this and put the past to rest. We called Renee a few times, and she assured us that Steve was a changed man, and he didn't abuse her anymore, But when Renee heard Tommy's voice you could tell how much she really loved him like her own son and when we told her we were coming to visit her, she dropped the phone and Tommy and I laughed because she was so excited we thought she had fainted on the phone I told Tommy some people mellow with age and as long as he doesn't abuse Renee anymore and they have found happiness somehow together it's all good, and at that time I think Tommy understood that! So, Tommy cleared everything with Big Vic, and told him that he was going to New Jersey for a few days and then his boss at his job which he took a lot of shit from, but Tommy told him this was something that needed to be done. When I told Adam we contacted Renee, and we were off to see the Cade's, he was overjoyed and knew that this would bring closure in Tommy's life! And I urged Adam If he heard anything about his producer friend to please update us as soon as possible. At this time, it really felt everything was coming together for us! So, we hopped on a bus from Chicago to New Jersey.

Saturday afternoon, Steve and Renee's house, Grant Ave
Nutley New Jersey.

Tommy and Felice had taken a cab from the bus station. The cab pulls up to a big beautiful yellow house, in which Steve required and made a sizable amount of money playing the stock market making a very

comfortable life for both of them and their child Nicole who is now a Sixteen-year-old junior in high school.

Tommy and Felice help the cabbie take their luggage out of the trunk and look at the house. Tommy stairs at the house, Felice looks at him, "Are you ready Tommy?" Tommy with the sun in his eyes continues to look at the house, "Yeah, I'm ready!" Renee, now forty-nine years old, still a stunner of a woman looking through the front door of the house comes running out and down the walkway to them both. This is like a dream come true for her. Renee shouts and hugs them both, "Tommy! Oh, my god Felice! I can't believe that you both look so great!" Felice hugs Renee tightly, "It's great to see you! It's been such a long time!" Renee looks at Tommy and starts to cry, letting go of Felice for a moment and grabs Tommy hugging him, as she does this one can feel the torment they have shared in the past together at the hands of Steve, Renee cries, "Tommy, I thought I'd never see you again. Nicole and I missed you so much!" Tommy with a distant, sullen look in his eyes, fighting back tears. Now at this time a beautiful teenage girl comes out of the house. This is Nicole, sixteen, Renee and Steve's daughter, she cries and runs into Tommy's arms. Nicole crying, "Tommy! Tommy!" Tommy starts to cry at this point. A bit ashamed of himself for doing so and looks at Felice. She looks back at him sadly, but with a smile. Tommy lowers his eyes.

Present day, Felice at the police station, Felice very sad thinking, "I've never felt so much sadness before in my whole entire life! I could actually feel the pain pour out of all of them at that moment. It was totally real and from the heart! What I saw that day, the way Tommy looked. He had so much pain and grief inside of him and when he had seen Renee and Nicole again, it brought him a sense of closure, at least for a brief moment!" Felice sits in the chair and thinks hard. She starts to cry and Sandy, knowing that the moment is too much for Felice to handle, comes over to hug her daughter. Vic, who continues to stand against the wall. Also comes over to Felice, looking at the police sergeant. Vic concerned, "Come on, sergeant. Is all of this necessary?" Sergeant looks at Vic, "Yes,

it is Mr. Levito," The sergeant turns back to Felice, "Now listen Felice, like I said, I can understand how hard this must be for you but the more information you give me about your past with Tommy the faster we could close this, and you can go on with your life and put the past to rest!" Felice thinks for a moment and then continues, shakes her head, "who says I want to put the past to rest? I wish Tommy was here right now. I would give anything." She wipes her tears, and continues, "Well, Tommy and I talked and ate for hours with Renee and Nicole. I never saw Tommy so happy with others at that time! All of a sudden...., the front door slams shut."Back to the past, The Dining area...., Renee and Steve's home,

Tommy, Felice, Renee, and Nicole sit around the table talking, eating, and laughing, Steve is not home yet because of a business meeting with his lawyers on an investment he is looking into, Renee had prepared him that Tommy and Felice were visiting and pleaded with Steve to start anew. He reluctantly agreed due to the huge ego problem he has with Tommy. The time is Eight thirty p.m. The front door slams shut, the four at the table know who that is and become silent for a moment. The whole mood of the atmosphere changes immediately from joyful to grim as Steve walks into the dining room, Tommy clenches his fists, ready if Steve makes a move. Felice, who notices this, grabs his hand, and looks at him, and shakes her head. Steve is now fifty years old well-dressed but has his shirt sleeves rolled up a very handsome man, very intimidating presence, very muscular, he still works out and trains like he still has a boxing career. Tommy and Steve's eyes clash, He walks over to the table, and he looks at Felice but trying to ignore Tommy, "Hello Felice, it's good to see you, you've grown up!" Felice out of respect gets up and hugs Steve Felice replies, "It's good to see you too." Felice looks at Tommy as she sits again. Both Tommy's and Steve's eyes clash again, but nothing is said. Renee, trying to make conversation, "You know Steve, Tommy and Felice were married just two days ago! Remember when they were young everyone said they would be, see fate works in mysterious ways!" Tommy stands up and extends his hand to shake Steve's, Felice, Renee, and Nicole. Look on, Felice holds on to Tommy's other hand. Steve shrugs his shoulders,

looking down at Tommy's hand. "Hmm!" Then look at Renee, "Renee, can I talk to you upstairs for a sec please?" Steve leaves the room. They all look in disbelief, except for Tommy. You can see the years of torment and pain rush back into his face. Tommy sits back in the chair, Renee comes up from behind Tommy and grabs his shoulders in total humiliation, "Oh, Tommy... I'm so sorry!" Nicole feels the same way, also feeling she may lose the big brother she never had a chance to get to know, and she runs out the kitchen door and slams it shut. Felice and Tommy are the only two left at the table. Tommy shakes his head, putting his arms on his knees, Felice grabs his shoulders Trying to console him, Tommy, we talked about this, whether or not this works out or not you still tried, you are the better man always have always will be! In a split-second, Tommy darts out the front door. And Felice runs out after him, where she meets him on the porch Tommy sits in a chair and Felice kneels next to him, Tommy looks out into the distance, "I knew it was a fuckin' bad idea coming here Fe! I'm just opening old wounds I can't get rid of for some reason, that mother fucker doesn't know who he is dealing with now, I'll put his ass into the ground now!" Felice trying to get through to him, "Because just with this situation you're stuck in the past. You don't need to feel like that anymore. I told you he can't hurt you anymore, I left all my pain to my parents in the past no matter how hard it was for me to stop blaming me! when I finally understood it wasn't my fault at all, If Steve wants to act like a childish bastard so be it! Your mind and integrity are all you need now!" Just as Felice says this, Steve comes storming out the door with his suitcase and jacket in his hand. He looks at both of them in anger, walks to his car, gets in, and drives off. Tommy and Felice just watch him.

Present day...., Police station,

Felice looking at the Police Sergeant, "It was hard because I needed to convince Tommy to stay for the sake of Renee, Nicole, and his own well-being for closer, but after that Tommy definitely wanted out of there, but I somehow convinced him to stay and Renee assured us that Steve was staying at a nearby hotel until we left in the next few days, It baffles me

that even Renee would live with such a person like that all of those years. Late one night for the next few nights I used my counseling skills to help Renee, she began to trust me and opened up about a lot of things she was a very good-hearted women, who was caught up with a very cold, disconnected person with no feeling, and she had been with him so long she really didn't care for herself much but understood the meaning of doing the right thing for her children, I really felt bad for her she was a young girl who wanted to grow up too fast and suffered the consequences for it!" Anyway, on the last night of our stay in NJ Tommy, Myself and Renee, were sitting in the kitchen having coffee........,

Past...., Renee and Steve's house, Kitchen, Renee, Tommy, and Felice have coffee, looking at pictures of the past, Tommy with much bitterness, "Renee, I wish you can cut to the chase here and tell me who I really am! No bullshit!" Throwing the pictures on the table, grabbing her hand lowering his eyes, "tell me, I've gotta know, please! It's killing me inside. It always has!" Renee nods her head, then gets up without saying a word to them. Tommy and Felice look at one another, and she returns with a shoebox and sits down at the table. She opens the shoebox slowly and looks at Tommy. Renee is a bit reluctant but knows this needs to be done for his sake, "Tommy, what's inside this box is what I have of your whole entire history, since the day you were born." Tommy looked intently at Renee, putting her hand in his, looking straight into his eyes. Renee was saddened, hoping this day would never come, "Your mom was my sister!" Tommy is silent, and Renee tries to find the right words to say. "Oh, she was beautiful." Felice sits closely to Tommy holding her arms around him, Renee continues, "But she could be quite wild, but she had the most beautiful hair and blue eyes you'd ever seen, and a personality to match, every girl I knew was jealous of her. Looking back now I'd have to admit it I was a bit myself it seemed she had men wrapped around her finger she did some modeling at the time and even tried out for the Rockettes in New York, she would have made it but she had a knee injury and that put a stop to that, she also had her sights set on Hollywood next but our father your grandfather put a stop to that saying "Actresses are

a dime a dozen"! and forbid her to leave! The hardhead your mother was didn't listen to anyone; I can remember our parents having fierce fights with her over everything." Tommy sullenly looks at her, "What was her name?" Renee looks up, "Jessica, everyone called her "Jessi" for short, we were all from Belleville, even your parents Felice, we had a tight click back then, something you don't see too much of anymore, then when your parents were married Felice it was like everyone seemed to go their own separate ways. They were the first of our click to do so and your mother Tommy was just about a year younger than me began to get really wild, staying out all night partying with only god knows who, she was only nineteen, Then he came along Bobby Cade a guy from the nearby town of Bloomfield, and just swept your mom off her feet, He promised her things that any girl at that age wants to hear a guy say, He told her he had connections with the modeling and acting field and that was the clincher she was his, anything to get her out of the house and into the limelight she was in! But soon enough, we had found out what kind of guy Bobby Cade was. He was picked up for armed robbery, assault, and battery, just all kinds of horrible things like that. Our whole family tried to talk sense into her, but the hardheaded Jessi shrugged it off like we were the crazy ones, like they say, love is blind! Soon things took a turn, and she found out that she was pregnant with you. Nine months passed, and you were born, I remembered your mom when she looked at you, she was so proud! She loved you very much! And she finally realized, looking at you, she had a lot of growing up to do, and she did just that. Our parents were very supportive, there was no If you are pregnant that's your problem and you're on your own, they looked at you and banded together for your mother and her new child! But soon after we got a call one night, and the police called us and said our parents were killed in a brutal ten car pile-up in New York state visiting relatives! Me and your mom's rock were gone, we missed them horribly, you were only months old when that happened! Renee shows them a picture of them. Anyway, your father Bobby was in and out of you and your mother's life. He wanted to control your mom, but she began to be too smart for his lies and finally left him! So Steve and I took you and your mother in to live with us, she told your father she didn't

want any part of him anymore but as she said this, he began to become more and more persistent and wouldn't give up on her, After many phone conversations with him, he finally convinced her somehow see him again, I ranted and raved but she didn't want any part of what I had to say! Then she somehow convinced me everything was going to be alright, her exact words to me were "I feel like a wuss, if I can't speak face to face, and she wanted to go alone and needed me to watch you!" She begins to cry, Tommy looks straight at her, "WHAT HAPPENED NEXT?" Renee takes out an old newspaper clipping and looks down at it. "After your mother got off work that night..." "And..." Tommy grew more and more frustrated. "Just tell me what happened next!!" Renee, her hands shaking, she continued to cry. "Your father took your mother somewhere in the woods in south Jersey, put five bullets in the back of her head, he made sure she was dead and then turned the gun on himself." Felice in tears, "Oh my god!" "When the police told me as soon as I heard that phone ring I knew and I needed to go and identify the bodies, Felice your mother was such a good friend, she came with to the coroner's office, I remember it like it was yesterday, that was before your mother and father started having problems in their marriage and months before they had you Felice, and I remember I had to take you down there with us Tommy and I held you so tightly in my arms at that time not knowing what to do with you I was scared because that was when Steve traveled a lot but I know I needed to keep you with me! So, this is the truth!"

Tommy sits there silently for a moment, then gets up restlessly, then rushes over to the table and slams his hand on it next to Renee, "WHY DIDN'T YOU EVER TELL ME THIS BEFORE? HUH?" Renee shaking from head to toe, "Believe me Tommy, you don't know how many times I wanted to tell you, but I could never find the right words to say!" Tommy yells, "That's why Steve doesn't like me. I remind him of my old man, right?" Renee doesn't say a word, Tommy with violence in his voice, "He thinks I'm a no-good bum... always have been, always will be, right?" Renee cries and shakes her head, "NO TOMMY YOU HAVE THE WILL TO CHANGE THAT! YOU ARE A MUCH BETTER PERSON! Our family has been plagued with

bad luck all of these years. It's up to you to change that!" Felice gets up nervously, "No Tommy, stop saying that about yourself." Tommy pointing his finger at Renee, "You made me walk around with my head in a sling about this for years just to tell me now?" Tommy, now in a rage, goes to strike Renee, but Felice gets in the middle to stop him. She screams, "No Tommy! Don't, please! You'll hurt her!" Tommy turns around and smacks Felice right in the face as she goes to the floor, he picks her up and throws her on the sofa. Renee rushes to Felice's aid, screams, "Tommy!" But then he pushes Renee to the floor, then turns to Felice again and strikes her again, Tommy to Felice, "You listen to me, bitch! You mind your own business! You don't know what shit I'm going through inside of me. Nobody does!" Tommy slaps her one more time. Felice screams to Tommy, "I'M PREGNANT!" crying, "WITH YOUR BABY! I found out when you were at the facility, and I wanted to wait until we were with your family when you found out! I thought it would bring everyone together." Tommy stops his rage, and falls to his knees in front of her, Felice gets up and stands there as Tommy hugs her, He begins to cry, Renee comes over to hug them both also crying, Tommy to Felice, "I'm so sorry Felice, I'm so sorry I put my hands on you! Never again! Never again! Felice, Renee, and Tommy continue to hug one another."

The present...., The Police station...,

The Police sergeant, writing this down, "so you believed him when he told you he would never put his hands on you again?" Felice looks at the sergeant, "And he never did again! I knew that wasn't the real Tommy, that was all the frustration he had inside of him, now we understood that family was filled with tragedy after tragedy. I knew I would have caved if I heard that too about my mother and father! You still don't understand, He had nobody, Renee was a nervous wreck, Steve hated his guts because of his father, all the immediate family he had besides members of E-6 Thunder was me, and I wasn't ever going to give up on him!" All the way home on the bus Tommy couldn't apologize to me enough about him hitting me, somewhere in between the time we left Chicago and coming

home on the bus, Tommy contacted Ashlie and the rest of my friends and get this set up a baby/engagement party for me if that weren't enough, they even went as far as having what the girls called the last true girl night before Tommy and I were married and having a baby weekend! Where we went to this great hotel all weekend and did girl things, it was fun, but I didn't tell anyone, but I missed Tommy and really didn't want to be away from him as foolish as that sounds! But we had a lot of fun! Tommy worked and had meetings with E-6 Thunder! We kept texting each other back and forth all weekend and I joked with him and told him he better be a good boy while I was gone, and he joked back to me and told me "I only have eyes for one person and that is you babe!" But the best part is when I came home, and Tommy bought baby furniture from the place he worked at and had the spare room we had and changed It into a baby's room! unbelievable he painted it yellow because we didn't know the gender of the baby at that time! I was really amazed by him. It was absolutely beautiful! We kept in close contact with Renee and Nicole through phone calls, e-mail, and, best of all, Facebook! That really made Tommy happy, and they always wanted to know the updates about the baby, so we showed them how big I was getting. I was so embarrassed and Tommy and I promised them we would get them both plane tickets to come and see us after the baby was born. "I know this sounds corny and all, but Tommy was a damn near perfect husband! And I tried to be his equal as a wife to him!"

THIRTY-TWO

Making Way For The New Generation

FLASHBACK Mid-Afternoon...

Tommy pulls up to a well-known jewelry store in E-6 Territory, who at one time was almost taken over by a rival street gang, and now it's under the protection of the E-6 Thunder. Tommy walks in the store and walks right up to the store's owner, whose name is Vito, Tommy jokes, "OK! This is a stickup!" Vito and the rest of his employees look up. In broken English, Vito says "OH! It's my favorite Hoodlum Tommy Cade! You almost gave me a heart attack!" Tommy laughs, along with the employees who are there. Vito comes around the corner of the case to Tommy, "What can I do for you?" Tommy replies, "What else would I be doing here if I need a ring? I got married a while back to a woman who counsels inmates, she's everything! And I need you to rip me off with the most expensive one you got!" Vito laughs, "Oh, Tommy you're full of play when you come in here you know I will never rip you off!" Tommy replies, "Then when I leave here why am I always broke then, huh?" Everyone, including Vito, laughs! Vito puts his arm around Tommy and walks with him over to a case, "So Mr. Cade is a married man huh?" Tommy nods his head, "Yeah, with a kid on the way!" Vito smiles, "Oh my God, Things must be good in the bedroom, yes?" Tommy laughs, "Of course! Hey, you dirty old man, instead of you talking about sex, aren't you supposed to be playing checkers on sunny days in the park?" Vito continues to laugh, "Oh Tommy, you always make me laugh! Don't worry, I still have it to give the Mrs. in the bedroom!" Tommy cringes and jokes around, "Oh God, I def! Don't want to hear about that! I need a custom ring of at least two and a half carats, round cushion cut diamonds!" Vito using his hands, "do you have a picture of what you want?" Tommy shakes his head, "No! but I trust you!" Vito nods his head.

Tommy looks in a nearby case and sees a jewelry box with a ballerina spinning inside of it, and says, "Man that would be the shit if that was a counselor that said, "Thank you for being there for me!" Tommy didn't think that Vito heard him. Vito looks and nods his head. "I can do the ring but I'm sorry it won't be ready for a while! And I will give you a great break on it." Tommy takes out a piece of paper from his pocket, "don't worry, I'm gonna need time to pay it off anyway, just as long as it's right!" Vito smiles, "You know only the best for you Tommy!" Tommy's phone rings and it's his boss. He looks at the number, "Shit, what does this ass have a tracker on me? Hey, listen, I got to get out of here!" Tommy opens the piece of paper he has in his hand and hands it to Vito, "And I need this engraved into the ring! Thanks!" Vito looks at the writing on the paper and raises his eyebrows, nodding his head.

Several weeks pass...

Felice, looking pregnant, is working at the facility with Adam as he counsels a hardened gangbanger with absolutely no feelings at all; he is around nineteen years old. Anyway, Felice gets her hours in, learning all that she can so she can become a full-time counselor. Adam sits at the table. Felice sits by his side taking notes down, the convict looks at Felice with a steady state, Adam to convict, trying to be down to earth and cool with him, "I've been working with you for months now what makes you do this shit? You have a rap sheet longer than my arm! Stealing, robbing and burglary, next time it's no more counseling here. You will be going to the Big House! Don't you know it's going to lead you down a road to nowhere? And then you are going to make me look bad, like I don't know what I'm doing and then I'm going to be pissed at you, Then I'm going to get in trouble! Then I'll be out of work, and I won't be able to feed my kids, and look at her she's going to have a baby, and she works with me, and if I get fired, she gets fired for not knowing what I'm doing, then her kid won't eat! Do you want that on your conscious If you have any?"

Felice sits there with a slight smile on her face knowing this is Adam's way to get through to his patients, The young gangbanger smiles and continues to look at Felice shakes his head for a moment and says, "I don't know about all that shit, But how do you get any work done with the most beautiful pregnant women I've ever seen sitting by your side all day long?" Felice not showing it but is quite intimidated by this as she looks at Adam. At this time Adam's phone rings and he looks for dawn to see who it is, Adam looks at Felice, and then he waves to the guard to take the inmate away, the guard comes in and takes the inmate out. The door shuts behind them, Adam moves closer to Felice, "You're gonna get that a lot Felice, don't be intimidated!" Felice nods her head, "I'll try not to!" Adam checking his phone again, "That was the call, Felice! That was my producer friend who just called me for Tommy's work! Stay here for a minute while I go into the next room where there is less echo!" Felice jumps up, "Do you think it is good news or?" Adam redialing his phone, "We'll soon find out! Keep your fingers and toes crossed." To Felice's stomach, "You too in there baby!" Adam runs into the very next room that is smaller than the one they are in now. In the door window Felice looks through and sees Adam talking and walking back and forth very intently, looking very happy. Felice smiles, Adam comes running through the door, "Felice It is a go! Tommy has a meeting with my friend in New York. I set it up. He loves his work and is very eager to meet with him!" Felice is very excited, "Oh my god, this is great, Tommy is going to go insane!" Adam laughs, "Well we don't want him to do that now he'll wind up back in here!" They laugh as Felice hugs Adam.

Nine o'clock p.m. The Apartment- That same night....

Felice paces the floor waiting for Tommy to get home from work to tell him the good news, Felice has the kitchen completely decorated with balloons that say congratulations on them and candles that illuminate everywhere! Felice hears Tommy coming up the steps to the apartment, and grabs a magazine and acts like she is reading, Tommy opens the door and sees everything illuminated in candlelight, and gets taken back

for a moment, Tommy walks over to Felice, "What's going on here Fe?" Felice very sexy gets up and goes into his arms, "Now, not only do you have a relationship with your stepmother and sister, Now not only are we going to expect our little baby in a few months, Not only am I not married to the best guy ever in this world, But now I'm married to the best guy in this world, That is going to be a produced on his way straight to Hollywood SCREENWRITER!!" Felice shouts, "YES!" Tommy stunned, "What?" Felice Jumps into his arms, "That's right! Tommy, I was at work today with Adam, when he got a call from his producer friend Mr. Ray Valentin, He had produced dozens of screenplays for a lot of people, Adam said he loves your work! And you need to meet with him, soon, you need to call him tomorrow afternoon!" Tommy is still stunned, "HOLY SHIT! I can't believe this is happening, I just wrote all of my thoughts down and it turned into a screenplay, I didn't even know what the hell I was doing?" Felice out of breath, "And he also told Adam If you have anything else he would like to see that also, Adam suggested a lawyer, to handle your affairs he said he will set that up and when we meet with Mr. Valentin, Adam would like to go with you!" Tommy grabs Felice and hugs her, "Shit Yeah! Is he crazy? I want all of you by my side, everyone who has supported me, through this shit, especially you Fe!" Tommy kisses Felice, "This may be my way-out babe!" Felice nodded her head, "Yeah it is Tommy, you said it!"

Present day..., The Police Station,

Felice shakes her head, "Ooh my god, what a time! When I say perfect, it was just that! In reality It was just fine but in the night-time was tough, I kept on having recurring nightmares of something bad happening, like a car crash, or someone drowning or a house collapsing on someone, it was the weirdest thing, and I thought maybe because I was pregnant or something I heard women get those crazy hormones, sometimes! So, I just dismissed them as just that! And I didn't want to bring Tommy down from this wild ride we were on together, so I just kept everything inside myself!" Anyway, the next day...,

The Next day One ten p.m.,

Tommy loads his truck with two other guys, he looks at the time on his phone and stops what he is doing and walks away from his truck to the corner of building, his boss comes with a business partner, "Hey Cade, what are you doing here, you need to work, get this shit loaded and out!" Tommy shouts back, "Yeah, Yeah, Yeah, just fuckin dock me I'm doing something important here!" waving his arm at the boss. The boss shakes his head, putting it down, to his business partner, "Just another asshole!" Tommy calls his phone and waits, "Come on, come on! Yeah Hi! Could I speak to a Mr. Ray Valentine please?" The Assistant on the other line, "Who's calling, please?" Tommy stammers, "Tommy Cade, he's expecting my call." The Assistant replies, "Hold on one minute sir!" Mr. Valentin picks up, "Productions Valentin here." Tommy, still stammering, "Mr. Valentin? This is Tommy Cade. Adam Quinn told me I should call you." Mr. Valentin replies, "Oh yes! Tommy, I've heard so much about you. I read your scripts, great work! When Adam told me you were a first-time writer, I couldn't believe what I was hearing!" Tommy doesn't care about the compliments, just want to get to the serious things, "Adam said you wanted to meet with me?" Mr. Valentin is very interested as he talks, "Yes, I do, and as soon as possible. I know I can work with your unusual style of writing! With what I read, you could go a long way." Tommy with a look of disbelief on his face, "I just wrote the whole thing from my heart!" Mr. Valentin, "Well I can Feel It "Tom!" I see you're from Chi-Town. Is that right, the windy city?" Tommy Looking down to the ground, "Yeah" Mr. Valentin, scheduling on his iPad, "It just so happens I have so much business to take care of out there two weeks from this Friday at the Hilton Hotel. I'd like to set up an appointment with you then, if this is possible." Tommy getting restless paces back and forth, "that would be great! Sir!" Mr. Valentin, setting up the appointment on his iPad, "Ok, that's the Hilton, I will have reservations at the main restaurant! Eight p.m. sharp! On the twenty-third, is that good for you?" Tommy nodded his head, "It sounds good to me!" Mr. Valentin, with Humor, "And Tommy? It's Ray! You can call me Ray!" Tommy hangs up the phone very happily, makes a fist, "Fuckin A! Ray!

The Present The police station,

Felice with a slight smile on her face, "At the same time this was happening, with the screenplay, Tommy was also out having meetings with Big Vic and Gatch and they told him everything was squared up, they were really happy for Tommy! It was so funny because Tommy said if he makes it big one day, he'd want Big Vic and Gatch to be his security. I was laughing, but Tommy was serious! They were all like my big brothers to me, anyway! They always made me laugh! Anyway, the big night was here, The Hilton Hotel and the meeting with Ray Valentin! As Promised Tommy wanted everyone from what he called his immediate family there, we had Adam and his wife, a very pregnant me, the lawyer who watched over everything." Thanks, Adam, for getting him. "Tommy wanted Big Vic there, but he had a prior engagement with his girl, but Tommy had Renee and Nicole there. They stayed with us for a couple of days at our apartment. We had a girl's day. The day of the big meeting, it was the best!"

The Hotel Dining room...,

Tommy sits restlessly as he awaits Mr. Valentin's arrival. He sits slouched in the chair, checking his phone constantly; It is already eight thirty-five p.m. Mr. Valentin is thirty-five minutes late for their appointment, everyone else at the table talks as Tommy thinks and restlessly gets up and runs outside without saying a word, and he runs outside. Felice knows of his impatience and lets him go. It is a rainy night as Tommy stands there; he takes out a small bottle of liquor from his jacket pocket and has some, then puts it back, thinking he was standing up at this time he is pissed. Tommy stands there for a few minutes, and a cab pulls up and a well-dressed man gets out. This is Mr. Valentin, age fifty. He pays the driver, and the cabbie pulls away as Mr. Valentin runs up the few steps to the hotel to try to get out of the rain. Mr. Valentin, shouting over the downpour, "Are you Tommy Cade?" Tommy nods his, "Yeah!" Both men extend their hands and shake hands. Mr. Valentin closes his umbrella, "Pleased to meet you. I'm Ray Valentin." They go into the hotel.

An hour and a half pass, dinner is finished and now everyone is on dessert, Tommy sits close to Mr. Valentin, absorbing everything he has to say as everyone talks with each other, Mr. Valentin, a direct person talks straight with Tommy, "Like I told you over the phone Tommy, I think you have a very special gift. A talent that I've never seen before and I would like to use it, you know... work with you. When Adam first told me about you, I have to be honest, I was skeptical about it. But when I read it, wow I couldn't believe you had no formal training in this, and I said to myself, how could this be? No training and the guy writes like this? Then it hit me... (tapping his heart) you write from here! Not like some other bozos who write from their ass! You have it! You put this, (Taps his heart) With this (Taps his temple) Into your hands and it turns to gold. You're the kind of person I need on my production team. It's not going to stop with just the work you did, we can go far beyond, I could see it! Adam showed me all the other things you have written. You're a person that only comes around once in a lifetime!" Tommy sits and looks at him, likes what he has to say but is not easily convinced, Tommy is unsure. "Well, you know, Mr. Valentin, you make it sound great and all, but I want to talk numbers before I jump into anything here!" Mr. Valentin smiles and shakes his head, and he pulls out from his jacket pocket a contract and a check for a large amount of money, "You still think I'm trying to screw with you huh?" Tommy hands the contract to the lawyer who sits beside him, and he reads it, Mr. Valentin smiles, because he knows Tommy is a smart he continues to talk, "Well for one, I have a reputable background, I've helped a lot of people get where they are today very successful careers for writers and actors. You don't have to take my word for it, ask around, I wouldn't want my time wasted and I wouldn't do it to anyone else." The lawyer cuts in and looks at Tommy, "Looks good Tommy! You're good to go!" Mr. Valentin continues, "All I want from you is a little trust! That's all." Tommy nods his head, "I know I got your M.O. already!" Felice sits on the other side of the table with Renee, Nicole, Adam and his wife, Tommy looks over to Felice locking eyes and gives her a wink, "like it's all ready to go," and mouths the words, "I love you" to her. Very proud of him, she

smiles back at him, and she mouths the words, "I love you too" continuing to stare at him despite everyone talking around her.

THIRTY-THREE

Paying your dues to the E-6

The Time is Eleven Ten p.m...,

Tommy, Big Vic, and Sal Blonde, drive down the streets of Chicago in E-6 territory, Big Vic drives the car, Tommy rides shotgun, as Sal Blonde sits in the back, Big Vic is very concerned and a bit furious, because the rival gang Diablo's crew tags have been showing up around in and around E-6 territory. Big Vic pissed off, "I'm sorry to you guys that I had to take you away from your women, but this is a major problem we have here." "WHAT THE FUCK IS DEABLO"S CREW TAGS DOING IN OUR STREETS? There up to something, I'm not surprised though with all this media bullshit, we're starting, we're drawing too much attention to ourselves. Those mother fuckers, might be looking for war! I need all of us to look out for one another! Those fucks don't play!" Big Vic stops the car in front of a tag, Tommy does a low whistle to Sal Blonde who is sitting in the backseat of the car, Sal covers up, "those fuckin pussies tags, they're making our streets look bad!" Sal immediately gets out of the car. Sal crosses out the tags with the E-6 tags very quickly and efficiently, then jumps back into the car. Big Vic to Tommy, "Let's take a ride, I need to see what they are up to!"

Present Day...., Police Station,

Felice shakes her head, "It was totally out of protocol for even Big Vic to go outside to search in enemy streets, but he felt that if they turned the other way and let these things go, it would start to get way out of hand, Big Vic felt it was a damned if you do damned if you don't type situation, one they didn't want to look like punks and back away from anyone and two if

anymore got out in the media there would definitely be hell in our streets! Most important, if E-6 went down, who would protect the innocent people out there? Sure, as Hell wouldn't be our Police department!"

Back to the past..., In Diablo's crew territory, That same night, there is an Eerie calm on these streets, as Big Vic cruises down them, all three guys have their colors on, also the three black and white bandanas covering their faces, one for the top, one for their nose and one covering their chin and neck. Very intimidating as they drive, Tommy, who is still riding shotgun, sits very low with his arm out the window also with a pistol in his hand out the car, ready if anyone comes close to them for hours the cruise the streets to no prevail. Big Vic angered, "These pussies must be hiding? Let's get back to our streets!" Tommy and Sal Blonde nod their heads.

Big Vic pulls away.

Present Day Police Department...,

Felice looks out, then to the police sergeant, "You need to understand, that was the first time something like that ever happened since E-6 had taken control of those streets, that's what really concerned Vic!"

THIRTY-FOUR

"Our little girl was born! Sent from up above,"

The time is Four Fifty p.m. A very windy and rainy day, Tommy was at work on the road with his truck and got a call from Adam's wife Diane, stating that while Felice was at work with Adam she had gone into labor And Adam had taken her to the hospital. And Diane had met them there, when Tommy gets the call he rushes there as fast as he could, and pulls up to the front of the hospital sees a valet tosses the keys to him takes out a few twenties and runs into the hospital as he walks into the maternity ward, he is greeted by Adam and Diane, they hug him, Tommy looks at Adam, and hugs him and says, "thank you so much for everything you do "bro!" Adam looks back at him, and smiles, "Don't worry about it "POPS!" Now go help your wife deliver your baby!" Tommy nods his head with a smile. And Diane hugs Tommy as he goes into the room. Once inside, Tommy is asked to put on scrubs by the head nurse, and he does so, then looks at Felice and rushes to her side! Felice is in a lot of pain, but very happy Tommy is there, says "Tommy!" Tommy, a bit nervous to see Felice in so much pain, replies, "FE, I'm so sorry! I got here as soon as I could!" Felice replies, "That's ok! I knew you would be here." Smiles, in pain, "I have a little faith in you!" Tommy jokes and laughs, "touché!" Despite her pain, Felice laughs. Tommy looks at her, "I love you FE!" The doctor comes over and says, "Ok Felice you're at just about nine centimeters, let's see if we could deliver this baby of yours!" Tommy and Felice look at each other.

Two Hours pass, And Tommy and Felice's little miracle whom they've named "Sandy" is born!

A while passes, and Felice is in her hospital room, with her newborn baby Sandy in her arms, Diane and Adam are there in the room, and Tommy

walks in and goes over to Felice and Sandy, "I called your parents, and they're heading out on a plane tonight!" Felice looking up at Tommy, "Oh, that's great Tommy! Thanks so much!" Tommy smiles as he touches Sandy's hand, "Only the best for my two favorite ladies in the world!" Felice looks down at Sandy, "This is like the best of a crazy dream right now!" Tommy smiles, "Let's see if we say that twelve to fifteen years from now!" Felice in a joking matter, hits Tommy in his arm, "Oh stop you! She's the most precious thing in this world! And you know she looks just like you! Don't you!" Tommy joking, "Oh, God a female version of me? God help the world! Oh, by the way Renee and Nicole called to wish us the best and they want to see tons of pictures of Sandy!" Felice replies, "Oh I wish they were here too, it's too bad they had to go back so soon!" Tommy takes a picture of Felice and Sandy with his phone, "I know! But in the meantime, I'll send them a shitload of pictures until I can get them out here again!" Adam walks over to Tommy and Felice, "Hey you two, how does this feel?" Tommy scratches his head, "it feels great. I can't lie a little strange but frigging great!" Diane walks over to Felice and asked, "Felice, Can I hold your little princess?" Felice replies, "Sure!" and hands baby Sandy over to her and the women talk. Adam puts his arm around Tommy, "Tom, can I talk to you out in the hall for a minute?" Tommy nods his head, "Yeah!"

Adam and Tommy walk down the hospital hallway, Adam just stares at Tommy and Tommy looks at him and says, "what?" Adam pauses for a moment, "You know what Tommy, you told me months ago that you were going to back off a bit with E-6, I found out through somebody a war might be coming with another rival street gang out there." Tommy stops and looks at him, "And I told you I'd try but I'm in too deep! I just can't turn my back on them, I'd never do that, anyway! And if I did, what do you think I can just walk away?" laughs, "They'd kill me for turning my back on them!" Adam shakes his head, "You know Tommy, you can tell me to go to hell right now and I'd have to take it, there's nothing I could do about it! Anyone, including me, would envy you right now, you have a great wife, a beautiful baby girl, and you're headed for superstardom with

that mind of yours, please man, don't fuck it up! You owe it to your wife and your daughter to step away from that life somehow!" Tommy replies, "I appreciate all your talk but...!" Adam grabs Tommy's shoulders and looks straight at him, shakes his head, and lowering it, "Listen! I Love you and Felice like you are my brother and sister, I just want you to live a long happy life man you two people grew on me like nobody else!" Tommy replies, "Well Adam I understand where you are coming from but my life ain't your life to live! And if something is going to happen to me raises his hands "It's in the cards!" and there ain't nothin you or me are going to do about it!" Tommy walks back to the hospital room. Adam watches Tommy as he walks away, feeling powerless.

Nighttime Weeks later..., Sandy's nursery,

After a few hours of Sandy being awake, and crying, Felice puts Sandy in her crib, Tommy looks down at her as she is fast asleep, He jokes, "Now Ms. Sandy do you think it's ok if "Mom and Pops" get a little sleep now? You know we're tired too! Or maybe that's too much to ask from you?" Felice almost bursts out laughing, covers her mouth with her finger, "Sh, sh, sh... Tommy!" Tommy smiles, whispers looking down at her, "I never thought becoming a father could make you feel this special. You know I give you a sense of becoming grounded in your life, Ya' know? She's out to be a handful already, but it's all good!" Felice looks at Tommy and nods her head with tears filling up in her eyes, looking at him.

Present day Police station,

Felice was thinking very hard, "You know it was the weirdest things sometimes, I looked at Tommy in times like that when he looked at Sandy and no lie be the gentlest guy! He was so damn talented with his writing! And then I began to feel he was leading a double life with the vigilant work he was doing with E-6! I could never get my head around that!"

Back to the past...,

Days afterword, Daytime Tommy at work drives his truck somewhere in E-6 territory, as he moves along, he begins to see E-6 tags crossed out with once again with the tags of Diablo's crew over them also, Tommy notices some broken windows in store fronts around. His cell phone rings, and it is Vito, the jeweler. Tommy answers the call, "Hello?" Vito, in his joking manner, "Hello Mr. Tommy Cade! It's your friend the jeweler Vito! I just wanted to tell you that this beautiful ring of yours is done and ready for pickup!" Tommy is trying to play but a little concerned about the tagging he has seen around the area, "No problem, I wonder how much you are going to rip me off for?" smiling, "I'll be right there!"

Moments later, Tommy pulls up in front of the jewelry store and goes inside, where he is met by Vito. Vito jokes, "Hey it's the man of the hour!" Tommy jokes as he walks up to him, "sorry it took me so long but I had to stop at the local bank and rob it to pay for this thing!" Vito hugs Tommy, "come here!" The two men walk to the back case, and Vito shows Tommy the ring, Tommy looks at the beautiful ring, "Holy shit!" Vito smiles, "Do you think your bride will like it? OH, I also have something else for you!" Vito takes out from behind the counter and takes out a custom box and he opens it, and it is a women's counselor resembling Felice sitting at a desk as it spins around inside saying thank you for being there to listen to my problems! Tommy laughs, "She'll love it! But one problem?" Vito looks at the ring, "what's that?" Tommy smiles, "This frigging thing is so bright, she won't be able to see it!" The two men crack up laughing, Vito cleaning the ring, "Oh, Mr. Tommy Cade you make me laugh!" Tommy, looking down at the ring, "So ok, what's the damage here?" Vito pulls Tommy close and whispers in his ear, "For you...." Tells him the price so no one else in the store could hear him. Tommy looks at Vito, "Man you are the best guy bro!" Vito whispers, "This is for all you guys in the E-6 crew and what you do for us! Come on, let me get you up here!" And he walks to the register, Tommy shakes his head, and walks behind Vito and whispers so no one else can hear, "Hey Vito, have you seen any shit going down around here

lately?" Vito points his finger outside, "Well yeah, last week I saw some bums staring in my store and harassing some people, and I went outside, and told them "What are you doing around here?" They cursed me out, but surprisingly enough, they just walked away! And you call the police, and they showed up hours later, like it didn't bother them. That's where our tax dollars are going!" Tommy looks at Vito like he feels sorry for the old man. "If anyone ever bothers you, please don't hesitate, and call me! You hear me?" Vito looks at Tommy, "I know! But this old man isn't going to let some young punks get to him! I can't call for every little thing Tommy!" Tommy looks around so no one could hear him, "No these aren't just some young punks, something is going down, E-6 don't know how or when but it's coming." Tommy pays for the ring and the carousel box that the ring goes into that Vito had special made for Tommy, "So you call us if you see the littlest thing!" Tommy puts his hand around the back of Vito's head, "You're a good man, Vito! Thank you for everything!" and Tommy walks out of the store, Vito looks at Tommy, smiles, nodding his head as he sees him pulling away in his truck.

A few weeks pass..., Night Time, Three thirty in the morning, Tommy still suffering from insomnia, is awake in the apartment, checking on Felice and Sandy who are fast asleep, Sandy is next to Felice in the bed, He reaches over to kiss them both. Then walks out into the living room and puts the T.V. on a local newscast is on in the background, Tommy gets a pad and pen and decides to write Renee, Nicole, and Felice's parents Sandy and Frank, Letters explaining his feelings and that he just purchased a ring for Felice and he would like them to come out for a get together, somewhat to make up for them not being there for their marriage. Tommy felt writing a handwritten note rather than calling them or using Facebook is more personal to express his feelings for them and, most importantly Felice and their new daughter "Sandy" also his plans for hopefully a bright future together. He also included on how he would like to try to mend his turbulent relationship with Steve somehow? As Tommy writes this heartfelt note, he stops for a moment to hear the news and notices that the newscaster is on a breaking story that two young boys

have been abducted from around E-6 territory a few hours before. Tommy stares at the T.V. for a moment intently! And gets his phone just knowing that Big Vic and Gatch had heard the news, and he would be getting a call for this at any time.

THIRTY-FIVE

Infiltration on the Grounds Of E-6 Territory

Sunday Afternoon... Twelve forty-five p.m.,

Five E-6 crew members, Big Vic, Gatch, Tommy, and two other members scour the streets looking for the two missing boys, Tommy rides shotgun to Big Vic, and Gatch and the other two guys sit in the back, all men not wearing their colors at this time to lay low from some 5-0 that will pick them up if caught delaying the search process for the two boys. Big Vic shouts, "I want us on this Twenty-four seven until it's done! You hear me?" One E-6 member in the backseat replies, "What about 5-0 Vic, you know sooner or later they'll come down on us for something?" Big Vic goes ballistic, "FUCK 5-0! Those corrupt fuckers! They want all this to end! E-6 to be done so they could control everything! Take money underhanded from the criminals they so call control!" Hits the wheel of the car, "MOTHER FUCKERS! If we don't take care of this soon, we're all done for! Not only us, our families, everyone!" As they drive, Tommy's phone rings. It's a call from Felice, with a picture of Felice and Sandy on the screen of his phone! Tommy looks down at it and makes it buzz for a moment, and not because he wants to, but he ignores the call and continues to look out the window like he's between a rock and a hard place. Gatch looks out his window from the back, "Look at this shit Vic, more tags over ours! But are they not marked? Just ours crossed out, what the fuck does that mean?" Tommy looking out his widow, "It could be Diablo's crew, working with another crew?" Big Vic nods his head, "That's right! Those cocksuckers are looking to do us in for good! If that's the case, we need to call everyone we can together! I really don't like this at all. We got to take control of this fast, but I don't know how?"

The present Police Station,

Felice Looking out into the distance, "All I knew is when I heard on the T.V. that an amber alert was issued for the two missing boys, my heart dropped for them and their families It spread like wildfire, all over Illinois, I haven't seen Tommy much at that time his boss began calling my phone, screaming at me asking where he was? I knew but wasn't going to tell him, so I had to say anything to cover for him! And I held him off until something broke with the missing boys! I had much faith in E-6 that they would find them somehow? But I prayed every second that I could that E-6 found the boys alive!" with tears. "Those poor families! I couldn't even imagine what they were going through at that time! Tommy had no choice but to tell me what was happening out in the streets at that time and what E-6 Thunder was doing to bring us closer to that situation! But he constantly texted me to see how Sandy and myself were and he said to watch myself and make myself scarce on the street because what was going down!" "So, Ashlie and the rest of my friends watched Sandy for me as much as they could so I could go to work! That was a very unsettling time, and either Adam or his wife Diane picked me up to get to work, to stay off the street as much as possible. I made some excuses for Tommy to Adam on why he wasn't there. But Adam knew where he was, and nothing else was said about it, and we kept at it! Most importantly I prayed so much for my husband Tommy that he would come home safe sometime! I knew he was street smart, and he had a good crew behind him and everything, but there's always that doubt." "What if he doesn't come home?" The Police sergeant, looking at Felice, "Why didn't you just take your daughter and just leave at that time?" Felice gets a bit upset with his question and replies, "For one I was never going to I was never going to just leave Tommy! And Two Just picked up my daughter at that time and ran! And three, nobody knew the severity of the situation at that time! It's called loyalty! I had people to take my daughter if I needed them too! But everyone thought if E-6 or anyone else found the two boys alive and safe, everything would have died down and E-6 would take control of our streets again!" Police sergeant nodded his head, "Ooh, and the boys

were found, right? Refresh my memory, E-6 did find the boys, right?" "Big Vic got a tipoff from someone within an affiliation of E-6, my husband was leading the set who found them! Those poor boys were locked in a crack house in an attic for weeks in Diablo's crew territory. Big Vic urged whatever set found the boys to watch each other's backs and be very careful because Diablo's crew fought dirty and they were always high on something! and it could be a trap! so he told all of them to get in and get out, as quick as they can!"

Felice drifts back into the past continuing her story....Tommy and eight members of E-6 Thunder run up the steps of a dilapidated crack house passed bums and strung out drug addicts, when they get to the top of the steps there's a door at the end of the hall, Tommy without hesitation kicks down the door with two kicks, finding the two young boys on the floor, blindfolded, chained up, and somewhat malnourished, with scraps of food and dirty water to drink. Again, each member is in full colors with their bandanas covering their heads and faces, Tommy and E-6 storm into the room, and go over to the young boys and free them from the chains and blindfolds. The one boy opens his eyes, though weak, but looks at Tommy, "Shit! I Told you Charlie E-6 would find us," get excited, "Yes I knew it!" Charlie is also quite weak but also gets excited, "Holy crap! It's them it's E-6 Thunder!" Tommy looks down and picks the first boy up, "Are you guys, ok?" The boy nodded his head, "yeah, we were just riding our bikes down the street and these guys came out of nowhere and took us there! They fed us a little but kept taking it away!" Tommy looking down at the boy, "well we gotta get you guys back to your parents, and we will get you something to eat! It's over now!" Charlie looks at another member of E-6 and says, "can I join E-6 one day?" E-6 member replies, "When you're eighteen!" Now the E-6 gang members take the two boys out of the house into their cars and back to safety.

Felice back to the present...,

Felice shakes her head. "You know it was funny, because after that incident, right after it was funny because the police department tried to take full responsibility for the recovery of the boys! But people wouldn't believe that crap, anyway! People couldn't get enough of them! Like I said before, it was easy to blame E-6 if something went wrong, because they were outcasts in a normal society. Then, when they put themselves on the line dozens of times in which they did, they didn't want or need any publicity for the great deeds that they did! They were so low key they didn't want any admiration. Just as long as their streets were safe, that was enough for them! They were one of a kind! But after the two boys were saved, the taunts against E-6 Thunder continued, by the Diablo's crew supposedly, word got around that they began to recruit many members of the smaller street gang The Killa Dogs and made a truce and banded together against E-6, which was a triple threat. So Big Vic had all His Members of E-6 stay as close as close to our streets as possible!"

Chicago city streets..., Dusk, Six fifty-five p.m. E-6 Territory "Thursday"

An unmarked car slowly cruises the streets, unknown to anyone, this is Diablo's crew leader named Derik D-Havoc Villa and a Diablo's crew member who goes by the name "Fire" blending in perfectly, well dressed, and normal looking guys. They melodically cruise up and down the streets, planning their assault against E-6 Thunder or whoever gets in their way. As D-Havoc drives, E-6 Thunder members on watch walk past them unsuspectedly. D-Havoc looks at them in anger, and says "These Mother Fuckers don't know what they're in for!" Fire replies, "When is this shit going down?" D-Havoc replies, "Saturday at midnight! And after we're done with these E-6 bitches, we're gonna turn on the killer dogs too!! I'm fuckin" tired of all this shit. They want publicity Chi-Towns going to get a full dose of it! I'm going to bring this part of the city to its knees!"

The Present..., Police Station,

Felice thinking, "For a brief time there for about a week maybe, there was such an Eerie calm in the city, everyone you talked to knew something was off, but things were quiet so Tommy and I took advantage of our time together taking Sandy to places. And when we put her down to sleep, Tommy made such love to me it was incredible! But all of that happiness was short-lived! Because no sooner did we have a sense of normalcy, that horrible Saturday night came! "WHEN ALL HELL BROKE LOOSE" in E-6 Territory!"

THIRTY-SIX

"All of Hell Breaks Loose,"

Saturday Night Ten forty-five p.m. E-6 Territory,

Outside is very misty, looking like the sky is going to open up at any moment, a few E-6 members patrol the streets, passing a high-end Italian Restaurant. This restaurant is packed with patrons at this time, a newly engaged couple and their friends are out celebrating this occasion, also there are their parents! The engaged couple's names are Phil and Kim, and their friends' names are Luis and Samantha. They eat, talk, and laugh, and Kim tells them what it felt like when he proposed to her on their trip to Disney World! Kim shakes her head, looking into Phil's eyes, "You never cease to amaze me!" Phil looking back at her, "Well, it's only the best for you! I was worried that you would have caught on when I made the plans to go to Disney, thank God you didn't! Besides, you did tell me that was your favorite place, right?" Kim, with a glass of wine in her hand, pulls his tie close to her, "Come here! Thank you!" As the two kiss, Kim's mother says, "Aw! What a couple these two make!" Kim's father raises his wineglass to them and says, "Gin-Don! A hundred years to the newly engaged couple!" other patrons from other tables and the restaurant's staff raise their glasses and clap for them.

A few tables away are two well-dressed men, who stare at the couple, not saying a word throughout what's going on around them. These are two Diablo's crew members, who have vicious plans in mind for all of them. They look and whisper to each other melodically, planning their attack on these couples.

At the newly engaged couple's table, Kim's mother and father are getting ready to leave, and get up out of their seats with Kim's mom. "I guess it's time for your father and I to leave and let you have some fun! Without us old people around!" Phil gets up, "No sir you can never bother us!" Kim's father replies, "I have to get up early for work tomorrow anyway, and another thing you can drop the Sir crap! We're almost family! Call me mike!" Mike pulls Phil over to him and hugs him, "Take good care of my daughter you!" Phil looking at him with a lot of respect, "I will Mike!" Kim gets up to hug her mom and dad, with tears in her eyes, "thank you so much Mom and Dad, I love you! For being there and supporting us!" Kim's Mom hugging her daughter tightly, "There's no need to thank us honey, your father and I knew you made the right choice from the beginning with Phil!" Kim nods her head and puts it down, "Thanks anyway! Oh, Mom, where are you and Daddy parked?" The mother adjusting her coat, "In the back! I think we parked next to your car!" Phil replies, "Do you want me to walk you out?" Mike Chimes in, "Are you kidding, this old man can still take good care of his lady! You guys just sit and relax!" Phil nods his head and sits down. Kim says, "we'll be leaving in about fifteen minutes ourselves; we are just going to the club for a while and hang out with our friends." As Mike walks out, he jokes with his daughter, "Oh, how many friends do you need? You'll have your best friend forever, sitting right next to you for the rest of your life!" Phil raises his glass to mike, "Thanks mike!" The two couples laugh.

Meanwhile... The two Diablo crew members listen to every word that was said, the one Diablo mouths the words to the other "In the back", and takes his cell phone out, possibly to call D-Havoc.

Moments later... A bottle of high-end champagne is brought to the table by a waiter, he turns to the men who sent it to them which turns out to be the two Diablo crew members, at this time unknown to anyone at this time. The newly engaged couple find it weird and nod their heads at them with a slight smile on their heads. And the two Diablo crew members smile back and raise their glasses to them with very sinister looks on

their faces, just like an animal stalking their prey! And one of them winks his eye at Kim, she feels uneasy, lowering her head and turns to Phil.

Ten minutes pass..., Kim tries to have a good time with Phil and her friends but still feels uneasy because every once in a while, she looks over at the Diablo's crew member and he looks at his watch, smiling at her and mouths the words, "Come on let's get out of here!" As he says that to her, she gets really frightened and turns to Phil and without getting nervous in front of him and their friends, "Hey Phil can we go now?" Phil at first talking and laughing with their friends not paying attention to what's going on, "Yeah Babe is everything ok?" Kim sensing serious trouble before it begins, "Yeah, I just thought we could head out to the club, we have to meet everyone else there!" Phil, "Sure babe no problem!" to their friends, "You're cool with that right?" The friends, "Sure no problem, Let's get out of here!" Phil asks the waiter for the check, Kim looks back to see if the two men are there but they have left already, the waiter comes back with the check, Phil now helps Kim on with her coat and now make their way outside to the back parking lot. Phil holds Kim close to him, very happy for the moment they kiss each other before they walk out the door. The back lot is quite desolate with hardly any cars and no valet, The two couples look and see about eight gang members, "Diablo's crew members" leaning on Phil's brand new Mercedes Benz, at first he is pissed, but common sense this is going to be trouble, Kim grabs hold of Phil's arm. Phil was leery but begins to walk close to them, "Hey guys please man, this is a brand-new car, you're going to scratch it!" A Diablo's crew member, "Oh, these are the two kids that are going to start a family together, huh? How nice!" Kim walks over to Phil and tries to pull him back as some members jump on the car and shout out, "ARE YOU FROM THIS AREA? ARE YOU FROM E-6 TERRITORY? Do you know who I'm talking about? Did you ever hear of them before?" Kim was scared, "Sure, we know who they are, but we don't have any affiliation with them!" Two members walk over to them one pushes Phil out of the way while the other pulls Kim close to him, "You are beautiful" whispers in her ear, "This could be like your bachelorette party where you get fucked good and hard

for the very last time! Before you settle down with this lame ass bitch!" All members of Diablo's crew laugh, Phil tries to pull away and they sucker punch him right in the mouth he falls to the ground, Kim screams, and they kick him, Diablo's crew member shouts as Phil lies on the ground, "You're a tough guy, huh? You know you don't have this piece of pussy right here, you know that!" Phil's friend steps up but tries to protect his girl and Kim. "Hey, look man, my friend may have been a little out of line with you guys, but can we just go? Please, we don't want any trouble!" He goes over to Phil and goes to pick him up, The Diablo's crew member looks at him, and feels his arm. "You look like you work out, huh? Are you a bodybuilder or something?" Another member comes up from behind him and begins to choke him with a chain and other members start to beat him to the ground. The two girls scream, Phil yells, "Please let us go!" A Diablo's crew member, "Yeah were going to let you go after we have an all-night party with you guy's, first we're going to fuck your girls, then were going to watch you two fuck your girls, then were going to let you guys fuck each other! Then we'll let you go to Hell!" Another Diablo's crew member laughs, "Yeah! We run these streets Motha Fuckers! Fuck E-6! Come and get us!" The head Diablo's crew member there drives up in one of their cars next to them and gets out of his car and goes next to Kim, "You smell so fuckin' good I have a hard on for you! Get these four bitches in the cars! I'm doing this on E-6 Territory!"

The Diablo's crew members throw the two beaten men in one car and drive off out of the parking lot where Kim and her friend plead for their lives, and the gang members put them in the backseat of the other car immediately begin to tear the two girls clothes off and proceed to rape them, as they pull out of the parking lot. All that is heard is sheer shrieks of horror from the two girls. In the other car in the backseat, Phil and his friend receive the beating of their lives!

The Diablo's crew laugh and spray beer on the two girls as members take turns on them.

All of a sudden, coming up from the opposite side of the road is an E-6 car with two members who at the time were patrolling the streets, not far from where this is all taking place. These two E-6 members' names are Bruno and Joe-Joe. Bruno drives and spots the other car as it drives down the city streets erratically! Bruno says to Joe-Joe, "Did you see that? That doesn't look right! Let's put our colors on." The two E-6 members put their bandanas around their faces, and Bruno turns the car around and slowly begins to follow the car's, keeping a few car lengths behind them Joe-Joe takes out his cell phone and calls Big Vic to tell him what they have seen. Both men sit low in their seats, so they won't be seen, Joe-Joe, "Yeah Vic, Me, and Bruno spotted a few cars heading south of Foster St. We think it is Diablo's crew tagged up fuckin' up our neighborhood! We're not sure where they're going at the moment! We got women screaming that it doesn't look good, ok, we will follow them!" He hangs up his phone. And says to Bruno, "Big Vic is bringing everyone he can! He wants us to call him when they stop, if they're heading down Foster, he thinks they're going to the abandoned warehouse grounds."

The same abandoned warehouse where Elliot Warner had met his untimely fate at the hands of Tommy and Big Vic.

Just as thought by Big Vic, they stop at that location, The cars slowly pull in, the girls are in total shock so there is an eerie calm at the moment, Bruno and Joe-Joe pull up across the street at first waiting for backup. Now the Diablo's crew members open the doors to the cars and throw the two women to the ground at first, and the men all are beaten and bloody. Bruno and Joe-Joe witness this, Bruno angry Like a true E-6 warrior, "We ain't waiting, they're going to kill them!" Joe-Joe, looks around, "Let's go!" Both men get out of the car and go into their trunk of the car and get out their weapons, no sooner do they do this they look across the street and see swarms of Diablo's crew moving into the lot and towards the helpless people, Bruno and Joe-Joe know they don't have a chance against all of them so helplessly they wait, Joe-Joe, angry, "Mother fucker's! they're going to kill those people if we don't do something!"

The young couples scream in horror as more members begin to rape the women and beat the men further, the Diablo's crew members urinate on the men as they kick and beat them and the girls scream as they make them perform different sex acts with them. As they do this, they say to the girls, "TO BAD YOU GIRLS HAVE TO PAY FOR ALL THE GOOD E-6 THUNDER DOES BITCHES!" They laugh. Throughout the Diablo's crew colors, there are also Killa dog members there also in their colors.

Now at this time as the Diablo's crew members are raping the women and beating the life out of the men, one Diablo's crew member spots Bruno and Joe-Joe, The Diablo's crew members stop and whisper to one another, then give a look to the lower gang members. The lower gang members scatter over the fences like they are fleeing the scene and the higher members get in their cars and begin to drive off this is when Bruno and Joe-Joe cautiously walk into the lot on foot, they have a handgun and a bat, and a butcher's knife, As the Diablo's crew members drive out of the lot Joe-Joe slams his fist on the hood of the car, "Bunch of Pussies" He shouts! Bruno, who has the handgun, fires shots in the air, and immediately goes to the aid of the two couples who are severely beaten and bloody. Bruno kneels down to the women at first "Kim", and kneels to her, "We're gonna get you out of here!" Joe-Joe, helps the other women up, and proceed to go to the car as quickly as they could, knowing that they have no time to spare the girls are in total shock Bruno shouts to Joe-Joe, "Hurry! there gonna fuckin come back!"

The two E-6 members did not have a choice. They knew they would not make it out but if they could help the people, that's what it means to be an E-6 member...., Do or die trying at all costs.

As Bruno and Joe-Joe help the girls in the car, they proceed back in the lot for the two men, this is when hordes of Diablo's crew and Killa Dog's member's swarm at them, Bruno pulls out his gun and starts to shoot at them hitting a few but not doing much damage. Now the two lone E-6 gang members are alone and, in the fight, for their lives. Diablo's crew

members and Killa Dogs begin to stomp on them. Phil and his friend are getting stomped on as well.

Meanwhile..., Valuable time is lost for Big Vic getting every member he could to the warehouse grounds, Big Vic shouts, "Try calling Bruno and Joe-Joe! Gatch! God damnit!" Gatch tries, but there is no answer. Vic looks back at Gatch, And Gatch shakes his head at Big Vic, "There's no answer!" Big Vic hits the steering wheel, "FUCK!"

In the car with Big Vic is Tommy, who is riding shotgun to Vic, Sal Blonde is in the back of the first car. With a total of fifteen carloads of E-6 gang members on route to the warehouse grounds, Big Vic shouts, "Those Mother fuckers got right underneath our nose? They're gonna get it now, it's go time!" As he drives.

But still unaware of the severity of the situation they are all going to face once they are there.

Tommy sits very quiet in the front seat, checking his voicemail. Tommy zones out for a moment as he listens to his messages. The first is Adam excited and happy, "Tommy great news, Valentin called! Everything is done, the funding is set, the actors are set, and the movie is a green light, and they will be starting the shoot in New Jersey! In October! And they want you on set! Can you believe this? You did it! Tom, you have it all! Beautiful wife and baby and now this! Man, I can remember the first time I read your material, this is no surprise you're going to hit the big time! And you deserve it! And we are totally proud of you! If you want to talk, give me a call later, okay? Take care!"

The first message is done, And the second Is Steven Cade, very mean, "Tommy, this is Steven Cade, listen and listen good, I don't ever want you to call here, send presents, or pictures of your family to my family here, or show up at my house ever again! You're a bad influence on Nicole and Renee!" Tommy looked very angry and sad all at the same time.

On the voicemail, he continues his rant, "You're nothing but a two-bid fuckin' hood. Always have been, always will be, you could hand me a million dollars cash, from that movie you wrote, and I would spit in your face! You're not my fucking son and you never will be, so don't let me hear from you ever again, or I will kill you!"

In the background of the phone call is Renee coming in from another room listening to Steve's vulgar and rude phone call to Tommy, In the background Renee screams at Steve, "WHY, WHY, WHY? Steven, what's wrong with you?" and he curses at her, and the phone hangs up. Tommy hangs up the phone and is looking down at the moment in disbelief and anger. Then coming back to reality and this situation from his zone out, and looks at Big Vic, driving as fast as he can and going ballistic, and shouts to his E-6 members, "WE GET IN AND WE GET OUT! AND WE FUCKIN' WATCH EACH OTHERS' BACKS!"

Now back at the warehouse grounds...., lower members of Diablo's crew stab and begin to strip the lifeless bodies of Bruno and Joe-Joe of their colors and hang them on fences while this is happening, making Phil and his friend watch this horror, One Diablo's crew member shouts, "Fuck E-6! It's going down tonight!" To Phil and his friend. As they lay bloodied on the ground hogtied lying on their stomach's picking their heads up off the ground, "We aint gonna kill you fuckers just yet! We want you to see what we are going to do to the famed E-6 Thunder!" They take kerosene out of the back of the car and pour it on Bruno's and Joe-Joe's bodies, and light them on fire! Phil shouted, "Jesus! No more, no more, why?" The few Diablo crew members who are there laugh, spitting on the bodies as they burn.

Meanwhile, across the street in Bruno's car are the raped, beaten, and bloodied Kim and her friend as they scream for help.

Twelve forty-five a.m...

Now car lights flood the whole area, as Big Vic and the fifteen carloads of E-6 Thunder arrive, not knowing the severity of this situation. All the E-6 members are in their full colors of black and white, also their Bandanas covering their faces. They get out of the cars, pulling their guns and weapons out; they see the two burning bodies of Bruno and Joe-Joe, Big Vic curses them! The Diablo's Crew members scatter but not before making sure that E-6 sees them, Two Diablo members go into the car trunk and take out two Molotov cocktails light them and throw it towards the oncoming E-6 gang members and then jump the fences some members rush to stop the bodies that are on fire out, Tommy and Sal Blondie rush over to Phil and his friend and kneel to them, Phil, beaten and bloodied looks up at Tommy, "It's a trap! They're looking to kill all of you! Our girls are in the car across the street." Tommy picking Phil up, "We got them don't worry!" Tommy and Sal Blonde take Phil and his friend out of the abandoned parking lot and into an E-6 car that was parked nearby. Tommy and Sal Blonde take out their weapons and go back into the lot and not knowing what lies ahead of them with their other E-6 crew members.

The misty night turns to a steady rain, Big Vic shouts, "Cocksuckers!" To some members looking at Bruno and Joe-Joe's bodies, "Put the fire out! And let's take them, out of here!" and he shout's, "YOU FUCKIN DIABLO BITCHES!" No sooner does Big Vic say these chords and chords of Diablo's crew and Killa Dogs members hit them from all directions encircling the highly outnumbered E-6 Thunder, shooting them, and throwing Molotov cocktails at them! Although now surrounded, E-6 tries to fight their way out, gunfire goes off between the rival street gangs. But Diablo's crew has complete control, and E-6 has no way out.

The next morning at six thirty a.m.,

The eerie rainy night turns to daylight at the grounds of the warehouse, and it looks like a complete massacre. Police cars, detectives, forensic crews, and the media and news crews are on site. Dead bodies lie everywhere,

the stench of fire still smolders in the air as firemen stop, the pockets of flame on and around the bodies. Many of E-6 colors lie next to their stripped bodies, it is so bad the hardest of civil workers, vomit amongst the fallen bodies. All of E-6 cars are parked where the members left them that night, doors and trunks open, retrieving their weapons for that battle. Except for Bruno's car that Tommy and Sal Blondie had put Phil and his friend in with their beaten and raped fiancé, that car was missing.

That same morning..., Seven ten a.m.

Tommy and Felice's apartment, Felice sits in a chair with Sandy in her arms holding her, Felice is watching the breaking news story. Crying, staring at the T.V. in utter shock after hearing the news, knowing what had happened to E-6 and Tommy being involved. Outside cop cars and fire truck sounds fill the air, also Felice's cell phone rings and rings but she does not answer it. She looks down at the daughter she and Tommy made together and cries, holding her tightly. Her cell phone stops ringing for a moment. Felice closes her eyes, thinking about the night he proposed to her when he was locked up in the facility, In Tommy's words, "Fe, I love you so much and all you've done for me would you marry me?" Felice replies "Yes!" They kiss. Now Felice's phone rings again, Felice quickly opens her eyes, and this time looks at the phone, it's Adam. She answers it sobbing, "Oh, Adam, did you hear? E-6 is gone! Tommy is gone! Oh, my god what am I going to do?" Adam tries to calm her down, "No! Wait, maybe Tommy wasn't there? Are you sure he was involved with it?" Felice shaking, "I know he was. I must have called his phone a hundred times, and he didn't answer, please help me." Adam was very concerned, "Where's Sandy? Is she alright?" Felice "Yes, she's right in my arms, I don't know what to do?" Adam nervous, "Don't worry about it, Diane and I have a room for you and Sandy to stay in until we find out what happened! Don't move out of that apartment. I'll be there as soon as I can get there. The streets are chaotic over all of this right now!"

Police Station Present day....,

Felice thinks, as her Father Frank shakes his head, putting it down, as her Mother Sandy has tears in her eyes, feeling for her daughter and what she has been through. Felice looks up, "After all Tommy and I had been through, I didn't even have a chance to say goodbye to him! I had a gut feeling that he was killed in the incident, but my mind played tricks on me when I stood over Adam and Diane's house. I kept thinking I heard the doorbell ring, and I would see Tommy standing there! But it was just a dream. Until reality hit and two detectives showed up at Adam's house telling me they discovered Tommy's badly beaten body floating face down in a nearby creek, they stripped him of his gang colors and burned fifty percent of his body, when I went down to the coroner's office, the only way they could tell it was him was by his Tattoo's! What those guys must have gone through that night, Detectives told me that they didn't know what hit them. They were severely outnumbered but tried to stand their ground anyway at all costs!" Felice's mind drifts for a moment to what it must have been like that night, pictures in Felice's head, show Big Vic and Gatch getting held down and beat by many members of Diablo's crew, Tommy getting dragged like an animal across the rubble of the warehouse grounds and being set on fire! As smoke plumes fill the air and a lot of shouting and raging going on around them. Felice comes back out of her thoughts, "Those poor guys! Trying to do good deeds for the community to go out like that." she shakes her head. At that time the whole community was really scared because there was no protection, the word around was that after the fight, there were E-6 members still around but without the core members and leadership of Big, Al, Gatch, and also Tommy the rest of E-6 soon disbanded and they were no more! Most turned to other street gangs, where there was no loyalty to anyone or anything. Who knows what happened to the rest of them? But was most shocking, when Adam and his wife took me back to our apartment and all around our part of the city, there were shrines, for E-6, their colors were everywhere it seemed Black and White! In places of business, houses, I even went past Tommy's place he had worked at, and his boss even had

E-6 colors flying strong! "I couldn't believe it." Tommy used to think his boss hated him, "Go Figure?" And when we pulled up to our apartment, Adam found it hard to step through our doorway, but outside were candles someone had left in front of our door for Tommy and E-6! That was so hard for me to look at as well. People even went to the town hall because they wanted to build a monument for E-6 right in the center of town, "Could you believe that?" "That said you are in E-6 territory!" But it was knocked down by the town hall stating it would have been an embarrassment for the police department at that time! The police sergeant cuts in, "I remember that! This is when this city was turned upside down, Like I said before, you couldn't tell the good cops from the bad cops at that time, the people got rid of the mayor, and pushed every crooked cop there was out of here, and started a new! Beginning with me! Felice, I personally will not make your husband Tommy or E-6 thunder's name die in vain! That was the purpose of all of this Felice, I knew it wouldn't be easy for you, but I knew it had to be done! Even though E-6 broke a lot of laws in the book, I could understand what they were trying to do out in those mean streets, and they were totally effective at it! But now it's up to this new police department to step up and get those responsible. I promise to you Felice I will get Every Diablo's crew member off the streets if it's the last thing I do! And put them away for life. This department just expanded its gang patrol unit and are on this case twenty-four seven until it is over with!"

At this Time Renee and Nicole walk into the Police station, With Felice and Tommy's daughter Sandy, Nicole holds her, Sandy is now Eighteen months old and the spitting image of Tommy. Renee Hugs Felice and her parents, and Nicole hands Sandy over to Felice's mother and then she hugs Felice. They sit, Felice with tears, shakes her head, looking at her daughter, "When our daughter is older and she asks what her father was like, I'm going to tell her that he was a selfless warrior of the Chicago streets! And was a solution to problems instead of being a statistic to one!" If there is one good thing that came out of all of this mess, Felice looking around at her family, it was bringing us all together as a family! Frank, now holding back his tears, nods his head as he kisses his

daughter's forehead. Frank to Police sergeant, "Officer, I think she told you all she can tell you; can we take her back now?" Officer nods his head, "Sure! There's enough to work with here!" Sandy cries for her Mommy and Felice takes her from Sandra. Frank shakes the officer's hand, and walks out, "Thank you, officer." Then Sandra, Renee, and Nicole, leave the room, then Felice says very sadly "Thank you!" and turns to walk out with Sandy in her arms, The Police sergeant, touches Felice's shoulder, "And Felice!" Felice turns around, "Yes?" Police sergeant, looking directly at her, "I know you've lost all your confidence in the justice system let alone our Police department, But I promise you that I'm totally on your side, and I will bring justice and closer in your life! Please believe me! For you and your daughter!" Felice nods her head, and looks at him, "I hope you do!" The police sergeant hands her his card, "If you have any questions my name is Officer Joseph Barns!" Felice, very sullenly, looks at the card and walks out of the room.

THIRTY-SEVEN

Redemption for E-6 Thunder

Two very long months pass..., Six p.m.

Adam and Diane's home, this very tragic loss has brought many tears this it also brought together a very tightly knit family unit, which includes Sandra and Frank, Renee and Nicole, Adam and his wife Diane, Felice's friend Ashlie, and her fiancé, and of course Felice and her little girl Sandy.

Felice earlier that day had received a call from the Police Sergeant now promoted to Captain Joseph Barns, urging her to watch the six-p.m. news that night, so Felice asks everyone to gather around the T.V. for a moment to see what this news is about.

Newscaster, Talks in a very serious tone, talking to her Co-Anchor, "And Tonight we the breaking news story everyone in the city of Chicago was waiting to hear for some time now." She turns to the camera, "The vicious Street gang Diablo's crew or Crew Diablo's key members where picked up late last night, Derik 'D-Havoc' Villa (Being escorted by police, through an enraged crowd of people) and was taken into custody and held without bail by the newly enforced Chicago police department also, along with Villa were one hundred members charged with the vicious massacre of famed but now disbanded E-6 Thunder, who just about a year ago intervened of a gang rape, and brutal beatings of two innocent newly engaged couples eating at this restaurant. (The newscaster stands outside of the sight where this all began.) This is where their nightmare began. The couples were harassed here in the back parking lot of the restaurant as they were exiting the eatery, then kidnapped and brought to an abandoned warehouse miles away. The two couples were then

viciously assaulted, beaten and raped by the members of Diablo's crew and possibly murdered if E-6 Thunder crew hadn't intervened on that night, who their key members lost their own lives saving the innocent lives of the two couples, stated newly appointed Police captain Joseph Bain, also head of the Chicago gang task force. We also caught up with the couple, who were brave enough to come forward with their chilling story and give us some insight into what it was like for them that night. The newly married Mr. and Mrs. Philip D'eara Thank you both for being here with us tonight! And giving us some insight with what went on that night. Kim, I can't even imagine what was going through your head at that time?" Kim with tears, "We were having a great time, but I saw these guys in the corner of the restaurant staring at us and they sent us a bottle of champagne but I felt that something was off with them and I wanted to get out of there as quick as I could, but no, I didn't want to seem paranoid and mess up a great time! Phil breaks in, "and that's where our lives changed forever! We thought we were going to get killed that night, if it weren't for E-6 Thunder, it happened all so fast, but I remember two of its members putting us into the car with Kim and Amber, and the car had the keys in it my eyes had so much blood in them I could hardly see, but somehow I got all of us to the nearest hospital, all four of us of course were worried about each other but somehow when I looked back I felt bad leaving the men who saved our lives but seeing how violent that other street gang was I knew E-6 didn't have a chance! to this day I feel guilty as (Shit) beep about it. I wish I could have done something, but I couldn't!" Newscaster nodding her head, "You do understand that you were up against something too strong and was out of your control. You are two of the bravest people I've ever met for speaking up about this." "Let me tell you!" Kim shakes her head, "Yes, but all four of us are still in extensive counseling. We both feel if something else happens to someone else, a true love bond will get you through any situation." The Newscaster breaks in, "Well, we all appreciate you both for stepping up and again being brave souls, would it be okay to have a follow up sometime in the future?" Phil and Kim smile, "Sure!" The Newscaster gets breaking information from her producer as she talks to the couple. One moment,

we just received word to switch to downtown Chicago. Where Captain Joseph Bain is speaking live outside his headquarters, "I have to thank Mrs. Felice Cade for all of her information she shared with me about her husband Tommy Cade's involvement in the famed E-6 Thunder crew! and for her trusting within me and our Police Department. And I hope that she could somehow move on in her life! So, we, the Police department and the many good-hearted citizens of this great city of Chicago, of whom E-6 Thunder once protected and lost their lives on that cold rainy night, would like to donate this plaque! (The plaque is in granite and is mounted into the stone wall of the Police Department, with the E-6 colors and sign in it, Also the names of the fallen members engraved in it) The people who stand there and cheer!" Felice Looks at the T.V. with tears and chills up her spine, Renee also sits by Felice's side with tears of joy, hugs her. Adam and the rest of the family also cry feeling Tommy's presence there with them Officer Bain continues to speak as the unveil the plaque, "This plaque is a warning sign also to deter any potential criminal who thinks they are winning the war with any vicious crimes and the new Chicago police department is here to say that we are here to stop it in its tracks. And keep the E-6 Thunder tradition alive!" "No more Crime!" People in the crowds "Cry and Chant" "NO MORE CRIME, E-6 THUNDER LIVES!" over and over again.

Felice, now looking at the T.V. crying, nodding her head, very proud to have been Tommy's wife and for what seemed like a moment having him in her life. The whole family, in tears of happiness, gathers close to Felice in support.

Weeks then pass, Felice makes it a very current thing to take Sandy to see the plaque on the Police station wall and tell her who her father represented and was. Sandy waves at the plaque.Months Pass... Tommy's Movie Premiere The phenomenon begins,

Hollywood Ca. A Hollywood Entertainment reporter stands outside on the streets of Hollywood explaining all the buzz and hype that is surrounding Tommy's movie,

Felice sits alone back in Chicago in her apartment in the dark in her living room, with tears streaming down her face watching this program.

The time now is now One fifteen a.m.,

The Entertainment Reporter walks in front of a famous movie theater as she begins her segment with the name of Tommy's movie surrounded in lights in the back of her, in just two short days, the much anticipated FROM THE DARKNESS COMES THE LIGHT, A STORY OF A BROKEN FAMILY, makes its debut. It's not a movie that has everyone talking but more so its writer, "An Ex Vigilante-Gangbanger from Chicago, Tommy Cade!" Who was brutally and viciously slain just over two years ago, helping the innocent. I recently went to Chicago to try to meet up with his wife Felice Cade, who had a lot to do with the authenticity of this movie, and I asked her if she had seen the finished movie yet? She said no, stating that It's still very hard for her to watch and talk about it at this time and she said, "I know Tommy was there at my side during the filming!" She also did state, "This movie will get through to people out there and it is a movie with a definite message, and she hopes it can change a bit of this hardened world of ours! And Producer Valentine, has taken other works from the slain writer and will produce them also in the future!" "See people, life does go on, and we do have a choice to do something in this world! I don't know if I'm supposed to say this on air, but I had a glimpse of the movie earlier today and I was completely floored by it! Not just by its array of actors portraying the roles, but the meaningful message it brings. I was completely touched by it, along with a few who had a chance to view it so far! (Putting her thumb up) Go see this movie. You will not be disappointed!"

The day of the Movie premier..., Nine Thirty a.m...,

Felice, drives with Sandy in the back of the car in her car seat, passes a huge movie theater, with the name of Tommy's movie in bright lights, dozens upon dozens of people stand in line to catch a glimpse of what critics are calling a phenomenon in movie making! Not for its array of actors or money content, but more so because of the meaning of it sent out to the world, and one man's view on which somehow tries to change it, for all to understand and benefit from. Felice stops across the street for a moment wearing a pair of dark sunglasses, and looks at the people, and says to herself for Tommy, "YOU GO GET EM TOMMY, TELL YOUR STORY!" Looks back at Sandy, "Your Dad Did a great thing Sandy! This may change the world, even if it's for a little while!" Felice pulls away.

That same night at Ten Forty-Five p.m......,

People come out of the movie theater being interviewed by the press. A man with his wife and two children are being interviewed. "This kind of movie only comes once in a lifetime! I'm thinking of turning around and going back in with my family and seeing it again right now! To see if there is anything we've missed! I can't describe it, it's not for just one type of person. It's for all people! I'm speechless! It's great! If you haven't seen it yet, go now, take your family friends, or whoever!" And now the reporter interviews a woman who is with her young daughter says, "this movie has so much heart. You actually felt the words pass through you, and you felt what the writer was thinking as he wrote it! I read somewhere that the producer took other works by that writer, before he had died, and is going to use them? I will be the first in line to see what else he had to say next time! (Wiping her tears) I'll tell you that! It's a life changer! Not from the money aspect, but it came from the heart! Fantastic!"

The reporter turns to the woman and nods her head, "that's what I felt when I saw it! It's a life changer for all to see! Learning from our

mistakes and changing them!" (To the women) "thank you!" In other entertainment news today...,

Months Later the demand from people, wanting to know who this screenwriter, the deceased Tommy Cade was, forced Felice to pen a book about him and who this worldwide sensation was. People were fascinated by her story, the book became a bestseller, with all proceeds going to different charities for children and adults suffering in different ways, whether from illnesses or helping people trying to leave gang life, and the impoverished! Felice eventually came out of the darkness and made her way onto the talk show circuit where she met every major talk show host telling her story about Tommy Cade. For much of the time, people could not get enough.

Felice walks off a stage after talking to one of these hosts, in back of her the lights shut down, as she walks her head is down, thoughts fill her head, "It took a long, long time for me to move on from all of this! But I knew I needed to, for Sandy's sake. In some way I felt that I did the world a justice by telling Tommy's story, then helping the people whom he wanted to help when he was here in life, I made sure all proceeds from my book went straight to charity! And I made damn sure Sandy was set for life and secured her future with some of the money, but she wasn't going to become one of these spoiled kids who has everything, and abusing it as she got older, no way! And still for myself, I stood with counseling as my best way to stay connected with others in need! I eventually became partners with Adam, and we run the same facility today!" When I look at the pictures of the people I've helped over the last couple of years, "That really gets me through each and every day, then when I come home and look at my daughter, I feel like I'm looking through Tommy's eyes again! That is priceless!"

THIRTY-EIGHT

Gone but not Forgotten

Six years pass...,

Since the demise of E-6 Thunder and the death of Tommy Cade. As time goes on, some tend to forget, and household names, faces come and go. But the Producer Mr. Valentine, makes sure with the help of counselor Adam Quinn that even after six long years people will not soon forget the name "Tommy Cade! And what the E-6 Thunder meant!"

Mr. Valentin had released Tommy's second screenplay to the world and became another worldwide hit and was about to release the third and final one soon. The media hype is insane, and people can't get enough of the story told by Felice.

It has taken a long time for Felice to come to terms with Tommy's loss, But Felice, now a strong woman, has met and fallen in love with a fellow counselor that works with her and Adam, named Andrew. At first Felice was very reluctant and not interested in Andrew because of her deep connection and feelings she had for Tommy, in which she told Andrew all about and he understood. But Andrew never gave up and pursued Felice until she finally saw something in him that was totally genuine. Treating her and Sandy with the utmost Love and Respect Felice has given out through all of her life. They dated and fell deeply in love and married and continued to counsel others who have had hard lives coping with their troubles in this world.

A beautiful summer evening....., Andrew, Felice, and Sandy now seven years old pull up to their brand-new home, movers are moving boxes in the house as dusk settles in, Felice looks at the house, Felice looking up

at the huge structure, "I can't believe we own this?" Andrew smiles and jokes, "We do and every month the bank will too! If we don't pay our bills, the sidewalk will look like a good place to live!" Felice hits Andrew's arm, "You're a joke a minute aren't you!" Looks back at Sandy, "Hey did you see that Sandy your mom just hit me!" Sandy Laughs, and replies "Mommy!" They all get out of the car. Andrew picks up Sandy and carries her inside the house, Felice runs to the closet. "I just love all of this space and these closets are just awesome!" Andrew grabs and hugs both Felice and Sandy. "It's all for my two best girls in the world, and by the way, I invited your Mom and Dad to spend a few weeks with us. I thought you would like that!" Felice hugging Andrew, "What did I ever do so good to deserve someone like you, huh?" Andrew looks into her eyes, "Ditto!" They kiss, and Sandy looks at them and says, "EWW!" laughs and runs away. Now at this time the movers are done, and the boss of the moving crew walks over to them, "Okey Mr. and Mrs. We're all done here!" Andrew takes the paper and signs it and hands it back to the boss, and hands him a lot of money as a tip. The boss looks at it, "thank you sir! Have a good night and lots of luck in your new home!" Andrew nods his head, "Thank you!" and walks the boss to the door, lets him out and shuts it behind him. Andrew raises his hands, "And that's it my love, we are officially in our new home!" Felice smiles and looks around, "Yeah but look at all of this unpacking we need to do!" Andrew replies, "Hey listen! This stuff can wait till tomorrow! How about we put little miss Sandy to bed, And I will run the water in our brand new jacuzzi? I get some wine and we have a great night tonight and we both unwind?" Andrew pulls Felice close to him, and she replies, "It sounds great, but you better be nice!" Andrew looks at her very intimate, "Ooh you know I will be I'm a bad boy with a good side!" Felice laughs, pushing him away from her, "Get outta here!" Andrew laughs and runs away playfully, "Let me go start our night!" Felice looks at him "Okey bad boy, you go do that! But just give me a half an hour. The T.V. is all hooked up, but I want to put our files in the right places, ok? Because we are going to need them for Monday, we're counseling that new couple!" Andrew Runs up the steps and turns to her, "One half an hour I give you! I will be waiting!" Felice laughs to herself, "Ooh my god, what did I get myself into

here?" She turns around and walks over to the T.V. and turns it on and sits on the floor and begins to unpack boxes.

An Entertainment channel is on at first Felice pays no mind as she is indulgent in her work, the reporter begins, "coming from Hollywood this week, top story coming from Valentin productions, is a biography of fallen mega screenwriter Tommy Cade! Called The Iconic Fallen Idol! A major buzz is that certain well-known actors are fighting for the role of a lifetime! The top spot!" Felice Stops what she is doing and looks at the T.V. The Reporter continues, Famed Director Simon Wiltch will direct and had these words to say, "Whoever gets this role has pretty big shoes to fill here, Let's just take a moment here this guy Tommy Cade died before anyone even knew who he was, but his presence is still felt around today why? Because of pure talent! You've seen the two movies, I had the honors of directing the first one and now they called me back to direct the third, and I also have the honors of directing the biography of this young man's life Hollywood didn't even know before his death, but left a tremendous impact on this world. It is a lesson learned to all of us, as you may all know I don't like to work with most actors and diva's because of their pettiness towards life, what I've learned from studying this fallen idol Tommy Cade is that is to don't be afraid to be who you are and help those in need and stand up for yourself at any cost! Things that we the living sometimes forget with our pettiness. I wish that I could have met him!"Felice's eyes begin to tear up but tries her best to stay strong and gets back to her work unpacking the boxes. Now she turns around and spots a box right next to her, which says Tommy and Felice, at first Felice doesn't know what to make of it, Felice dumbfounded, "What? Where did this come from?" She gets the box and pulls it over to her, and opens the taped up box, and begins to open it, she goes through a couple of articles of clothing belonging to them at that time, she begins to well up with tears afraid of what else she may find, she gets to the bottom and discovers a picture of herself, Tommy and Sandy at the time of her birth and a beautifully wrapped box she opens it and discovers the ring with a counselor sitting at her desk twirling around it. Inscribed around it is,

"YOU CAN ACCOMPLISH THE WORLD!" Tommy meant to give it to her a few nights before he had died along with a note telling her how much she has meant to her, and she was his rock and that he cherished his new family and start a new beginning with her and Sandy. Felice quietly breaks down at this time... She now looks to the other side of the room, nearest the T.V. is a sofa. Felice sees a vision of Tommy who is sitting there looking at her, and says, "WE DID IT FE! WE REALLY DID IT!" Putting his head down and he vanishes, and she cries, "Tommy, Tommy, covers her mouth!" She sits there for a moment, nods her head, gets up, and walks away. The ring is still spinning in the box.

ABOUT THE AUTHORS

Marc Saporito

Marc Saporito, born and raised in New Jersey, began his career as a screenwriter at age 16, all starting with a dream he had one night and created the first draft of New Dawning. When life intervenes and does what it does, he was forced to put his dreams on hold for a while until late 2011, when through the advice of a friend was encouraged to write his first novel, which became New Dawning. Soon after, he began to write the sequel to this hard-hitting story. Today Marc has written dozens of manuscripts that he would like to share with others. Not only other novels but screenplays; another is a Si-Fi screenplay movie trilogy which has now turned into a three-part comic book series. Always an underdog, I can relate to anyone who has tried and failed countless times, but you must keep rolling through the bad times to get to the good!! Don't stop no matter what life may throw at you!!!

Daniel Russomano

Daniel Russomano was born in Newark, New Jersey, and now resides in Nutley, New Jersey. He has a son Daniel, a daughter-in-law Lindsey, a granddaughter Mila, and another granddaughter Paige on the way!!! He has a French Bulldog named Rocky and a Parakeet named Angel!!! Who are best friends. He likes spending time with his family and pets, but most of all, he likes spending quality time with his granddaughter Mila!! And he is waiting for the arrival of his granddaughter Paige. He likes to garden, read, and go fishing. He has been friends with Marc Saporito for years and has collaborated to bring this hard-hitting and exciting novel New Dawning to the masses!!!